Praise for

Flash Gang

"Packed with clever twists and ever-rising stakes, *The Adventures of the Flash Gang* is a bright flare of fun, a throwback gangster caper with irresistible kid sleuths and loads of page-turning action."

—Ben Guterson, author of the award-winning *Winterhouse* series and *The Einsteins of Vista Point*

"Delightfully Dickensian in spirit. Period events are woven seamlessly into this rollicking tale of friendship and fortitude. I challenge any reader not to fall in love with the histrionics and devil-may-care verve of Pearl Alice Clavell and her grease-smeared partner in crime, Lewis Carter."

—J.R. Potter, author of *Thomas Creeper and the Gloomsbury Secret*

"Clever, catchy dialogue and non-stop action catapult the reader from page to page till we land breathless, intrigued, and anxiously awaiting the Flash Gang's next adventures."

—Kimberly Behre Kenna, author of *Artemis Sparke and the Sound Seekers Brigade*

THE ADVENTURES OF THE FLASH GANG

EPISODE ONE: EXPLODING EXPERIMENT

M. M. Downing and S. J. Waugh

Fitzroy Books

Published by Fitzroy Books
An imprint of
Regal House Publishing, LLC
Raleigh, NC 27605
All rights reserved

https://fitzroybooks.com
Printed in the United States of America

ISBN -13 (paperback): 9781646033225
ISBN -13 (epub): 9781646033232
Library of Congress Control Number: 2022935698

Interior by Lafayette & Greene
Cover images and design © by C. B. Royal

Regal House Publishing, LLC
https://regalhousepublishing.com

Printed in the United States of America

Contents

For Cece & Anna – M. M. Downing

For Christopher & Jeremy – S. J. Waugh

1

THE STREETER

Eleven-year-old Lewis Carter sat scrunched between a wall and a giant pickle barrel at Knoertzer's Pittsburgh Grocery. The spot was sticky and stank of vinegar, but he could see the whole shop from there—small and square, with a hodge-podge of tinned goods, loose vegetables, and specialty meats crammed onto shelves and counters and in bins. To Lewis, who hadn't eaten since the day before, everything looked delicious. It was nearly dinnertime, and for the past ten minutes he'd been planning assorted meals in his head using everything but the pickles: baloney on Wonder Bread, steamed cabbage with fried eggs, Saltines and sardines…his mouth watering with each combination.

Customers shuffled past. Some wore snug overcoats; some wore the haggard expressions of sorry times. None of them noticed Lewis. He was just another scrawny, pale boy with unkempt hair and threadbare clothes, lingering inside to cheat the cold. Lewis looked like what he was, what he had been for exactly one hundred and fourteen days: a streeter. And, except for his eyeglasses, he was as forgettable as any other streeter in the chilly March of 1935.

Streeter, not *orphan.* There was a distinction. Orphans were swept into charities, buttoned into gray uniforms, and bunked in gray dormitories that smelled of pine disinfectant. Streeters, on the other hand, devised their own shelters and their own methods of survival. And whether they worked in groups or operated alone, all streeters preferred to pinch a meal, to sleep under the stars with frost chewing their fingertips, than to be lost to a grim institution.

Besides, Lewis Carter wasn't an orphan. His father was just temporarily missing.

He peeled his sleeve from the brine-stained wall again and sighed. He'd been patiently waiting for the perfect moment but now his stomach was growling ferociously. Mrs. Knoertzer squeezed by for a third time, straightening jars and dusting shelves. Mr. Knoertzer stood behind the meat counter not ten feet away, waving frankfurter links while he chatted with customers. Lewis added hot dogs and baked beans to his imaginary menu and his stomach growled some more.

Then suddenly, the moment arrived. Mr. Knoertzer set down the wieners and lifted a round of sausage, presenting it like a proud papa and generously calling out, "Free tastes!" The grocer began carving tissue-thin slices of the meat, as what seemed like the entire store rushed to the counter. Lewis stayed where he was, his mouth curving into a smile. Finally, he could begin.

Working quickly, Lewis pulled a scrap of handkerchief from his jacket and laid it on his knee. From the jacket's left-side pocket, he took a pouch that held what looked like a tablespoon of sludge. It was thick, sticky, and black. Lewis smeared some on the handkerchief.

Next came a sort of ashy material, like the remains of a paper fire, from the pouch in the jacket's right-side pocket. He measured the ash by feel, sprinkling it over the sludge.

An off-duty copper hustled by, heading for the meat counter. Lewis held still until the officer passed, then reached down and ran his fingers along the floor, scraping up a bit of dirt. He removed his eyeglasses, rubbed the dirt on the lenses, and put them back on. Then he folded up the hand-kerchief scrap, gave it a good squeeze, and dropped it on the floor.

Lewis now had twenty whole seconds. He wiped his hands on his knees, then stood up and stepped into the aisle, pretending to study the canned soups. Mr. Knoertzer was cracking jokes about liverwurst. The copper was in front of the grocer, cramming sausage slices into his mouth.

Ten seconds gone. Excitement tingled into Lewis's fingers and toes. Now came the best part.

Ten…nine…eight…

Casually, Lewis reached for a burlap sack that was folded over a mound of onions in a wicker basket. He slid it from the pile and rolled it in his fists. Then he squinted through the dirt smudges, scanning for just the right spot.

Seven…six…five…

There: a bin brimming with oranges, just steps from the meat counter with its sumptuous display. Lewis maneuvered between the two and stopped, right next to the copper.

Four…three…

He nodded politely at the officer, who was reaching for another slice of sausage…

Two…

then grinned wide.

One!

First came a small *whoosh* followed by a soft *pop.* And then burst the most dazzling flare of light, expanding like an enormous umbrella, brighter than a hundred flashbulbs. Everyone in the shop froze until…

"It's the Flash Gang!" Mrs. Knoertzer screamed at the top of her lungs.

The gasps came fast and furious. "No!" "Where?" "Quick! Can you see them?" "See them? Try and catch them!"

"Out of the way, I've got 'em!" the copper barked, then ran blindly into the pickle barrel, knocking down several customers like dominoes. There were *oof*s and *ow*s and people tripping over each other. Meanwhile, Lewis, whose smeared glasses shaded the glare, was gleefully packing the sack full of sausage and cheese, then oranges and cabbage and mustard jars and loose potatoes. Food for him, food for the soup

kitchen at St. Patrick's. A pungent smell of rotten eggs per-
meated the dazzle. People were covering their mouths and
noses between cheering; the bell on the front door was jan-
gling; Lewis didn't pay any mind. Stuffing, stuffing, stuffing
the sack, and then walking—not running—through the shop.
And also, not coughing. That part required a distinct re-
solve.

Mr. Knoertzer was beside himself. "Flash Gang! It's the
Flash Gang! Call the *Post-Gazette!* The *Sun!*"

Lewis exited into a burst of cold air, which briefly
knocked the grin from his face. He coughed and cleared his
throat and then pushed through the crowd that was already
pressing in—plucky streeters, wealthy crusts, and everyone
in between, all rushing toward the umbrella of light. Mrs.
Knoertzer threw herself like a tarp over the bins of vegetables outside the store to keep her wares from being knocked
over. She was screeching in bursts, "Flash Gang! Here! They
chose our shop!"

They. Lewis could have laughed out loud.

Across the busy intersection was a tailor shop. Lewis
aimed for it, wedging himself inside the triangle-shaped folding board by its door advertising "2 Suits $20." He sorted out
his knees and feet, cleared his lungs properly, and wiped the
dirt from his eyeglasses. Then he pulled a sausage from the
sack and settled down to watch the hubbub.

And what a hubbub! A police van screeched to a stop in
front of the grocery. Coppers jumped out without shutting
their doors, causing an immediate traffic jam. To the left
and right drivers started honking. Passersby climbed on the
hoods of the idling vehicles to watch the frenzy. Mothers
yelled at their children to come away from the madness. Mr.
Knoertzer plowed out of the shop, ecstatic. "It's there! The
blue smudge! On the floor by the pickle barrel! That's our
proof! What luck!"

Lewis chuckled and bit into the sausage. He closed his

eyes for a moment in pure bliss. The fatty, salty chewiness; nothing tasted so delicious. A piece of cheese and an orange quickly followed. And then more sausage. This was almost as good as when his father splurged on two tickets and popcorn so they could see *Tarzan the Ape Man*.

"Psst! Brain! Is that you?"

Lewis jerked upright. He swallowed the mouthful, wiped his face, then poked his head cautiously out of the triangle. There, over to the left, were two boys his age squatting behind a metal mailbox. Lewis relaxed. Beak-nosed Mac and wiry-haired Duck were long-time streeters who worked together and pinched the usual way, with speed and nimble fingers. They managed to turn up almost every time Lewis set a Flash.

Lewis held up a jar of mustard. "Only left you some scraps," he joked. "You're late."

"We ain't late! Yer early!" Mac shot back. He was the smaller, jittery, and more thin-skinned of the pair. "Did you see 'em in there, Brain?"

"Who?" Lewis asked innocently.

"The Flash Gang!"

"I did!" chirped Duck, all proud. "They ran out the side there. Five big burly types, with special lightning wicks they must've got from Fat Joe."

Fat Joe! Lewis bit the inside of his lip. "You think the mob's bankrolling the Flash Gang?"

"Yep! They bankroll everyone—the coppers, the trash collectors. Anyhow, I saw 'em!" Duck returned loftily, puffing out his chest by sticking his hands inside the bib of his many-pocketed overalls.

"Did not!" Mac socked Duck in the arm, who deflated with a grin. "Told ya, it was pro'lly Knoertzer himself. Smoosh a beet on the floor, light a firecracker, and bang! You say it's the Flash Gang to get yerself in the papers and charge everyone to see it. Get rich."

"What about the rotten egg smell, though?" Lewis asked, biting his lip again to keep from laughing. This was part of the fun—hearing people talk about the Flash Gang without ever once guessing the gang was just one fairly harmless boy.

Mac was stumped. "Well, uh—"

Lewis let him off the hook by pointing across the street. "Anyway, looks like ol' Knoertzer's wish is coming true."

The boys turned to watch as a dented Buick nudged its way alongside the police van and stopped. Lewis recognized the vehicle and the man who hopped from it clutching a notepad, his dog-eared ID sticking from the brim of his trilby. It was the reporter from the *Pittsburgh Post-Gazette*. He'd shown up the last three times Lewis had set his Flash.

The reporter approached the grocer, who began an exaggerated retelling, thrusting and swiping at the air as he raved. Then Mrs. Knoertzer cupped her hands to her mouth and shrieked from the doorway, "Come see the smudge! One penny!" Almost immediately, a line began to form.

"Told ya," said Mac, socking Duck again. "Rich."

"A penny! Forget that!" Duck winked at Lewis. And just like that, he was gone, zigzagging across the street toward a darkened passageway at the side of the grocery. Duck was tall for his age but could whisk anywhere without being seen. He parked himself by the grocer's coal chute, mere inches behind three coppers idly watching the crowd, and waved at Lewis and Mac.

Mac looked over at Lewis. "You wanna come?"

Lewis's heart gave a little leap at the offer, but he squashed it down. Joking with Mac and Duck was fun, but he needed to keep to himself. He couldn't arouse any suspicion that he was, in fact, the Flash Gang.

Besides, his lungs were weak. They shut tight when he ran, fizzed when he got anxious, and burned sometimes when he was walking. There was no way he could keep up with their speed.

"I've been already, remember?" Lewis answered heartily instead, waving the mustard. "You be careful though with those coppers."

"They don't scare me," Mac scoffed. Still, Mac chewed his thumb for a nervous moment before charging to where Duck waited, vaulting over his friend's shoulders and sliding straight down the coal chute. Duck stuck his tongue out at the oblivious coppers and followed him into the grocery's basement.

Lewis waited another minute, then crawled out from between the folding sign and considered his hefty sack. He often made anonymous contributions to St. Patrick's soup kitchen as thanks for the meals they served those first nights he was on his own. Tonight's contribution would be large. Lewis stuffed the sack underneath his jacket and just barely managed to button it. If anybody bothered looking, they'd see a skinny kid with a hugely unnatural bulge at his waist.

But nobody bothered. Everyone was either pushing to join the blue smudge line or listening to Mr. Knoertzer recount the adventure to the reporter.

Lewis smiled. Nope, nobody would notice him, not at all.

2

Chased by a Bulldog

Lewis walked along Penn, still smiling. The avenue stretched from downtown where the Allegheny and Monongahela rivers merged with the mighty Ohio all the way eastward, so it was quite a smile. And even though frost bit his ears and the thick smog of Pittsburgh settled in his lungs like soggy grit, the smile didn't fade. Lewis's belly was full, and he'd once again gotten away with a score.

He replayed the scene in his head: the jubilation and confusion and frenzy and excitement. When the Flash Gang struck, Lewis thought (a bit smugly), everybody came out ahead. The Knoertzers would cash in on their blue smudge, the neighbors and passersby now had a Flash Gang story to tell, and streeters were always happy for a chance to line their pockets.

Yep! All in all, a fine evening. Too chilly perhaps, and hazy, definitely. But Lewis was pleased, even walking past all the scrawny dogs and makeshift shelters. One thin little girl sat on the curb twirling a piece of string.

Lewis fetched an orange from the sack and handed it to her.

"Where'd you get that?" Her dirty cheeks lifted in a smile and Lewis brought a finger to his lips. She nodded at him gravely and he slipped away before any grown-ups saw.

Almost everybody these days, excepting crusts with their warm clothes, plentiful pantries, and shiny cars, was suffering. Most businesses had slowed or closed completely. Even the coal mines and the great steel mills had to lay off workers. And Pittsburgh was a steel city, smokestacks lining the rivers, belching out dark clouds day and night, turning ore into steel. Now nearly a quarter of all the Pittsburgh folks were jobless or homeless or hungry, and many were all three.

Yet here he was, Lewis Carter, not knowing where or why his dad had gone and having been booted from their apartment by an uncaring landlady, managing just fine on his own. He wasn't slick like Duck or crafty like Mac; he couldn't run or jump without his lungs firing up, and he couldn't go to school because some busybody would learn of his missing dad and lack of address and go all out making him a charity case.

But Lewis still had one very important thing: himself. He had his wits, he had the ability to blend in, and he had his Recipe. And that was enough. More than enough. He was doing so grand, in fact, he could pay back the charity that was given to him and then some.

And that brought Lewis past the broad steps and columns of St. Patrick's church and around to the rectory door. It sat locked and quiet for the night; he could go in through the church, which was always open, but he preferred to keep out of sight. Lewis looked left and right, and seeing nobody, quickly unpacked canned foods and fresh fruit, the mustard, and a few onions. He made sure to keep what he needed for the week—a loaf of bread, the remaining sausage, three cans of beans, and a half dozen oranges—whispered a thank-you to the church and its soup kitchen, and then slunk off into the smoggy darkness. He was as near-invisible as before. A group of grimy, huddling men heated their hands over a trash-can fire, where headlines like "Grain Prices Fall" and "Hitler Drafts 500,000 for German Army" blazed to ash. They didn't even raise their heads to look.

Lewis was doubling back down Penn, a few blocks from the church, when he felt a tingling around the base of his neck and shoulders that wasn't from the cold. *This is new,* he thought, curious. Was he being followed? He stopped and,

pretending to tie his shoe, peered into the smog, back toward
the church. Nothing. He shook off the tingly sensation. Nobody had witnessed him at the church. And if it was one of
those hungry trash-can men, well, all they'd have to do was
ask. Lewis would share his loot.

He began walking again, but then the tingly feeling came
back, stronger this time. Something was definitely out there.
Something that didn't want to be seen.

Well, then Lewis didn't want to be seen. He kept his
pace for nearly a block, then slipped between two boarding
houses into a dead-end alley. He went for the sagging fire
escape, thinking how Duck and Mac would approve of this
clever hiding spot. The rungs were slippery, but he hoisted
himself and the sack to the first landing and crouched next
to a curtained window.

Lewis watched the entrance of the alley. For a moment it
was quiet; then, sure enough, something did appear. It was
a man, thick and sturdy like a bulldog, with a paunch that
strained the gold buttons on his green three-piece suit. He
didn't look like a squatter: too dressed. Nor did he look like
a copper, or the reporter, or any of the crowd who'd been at
the grocery.

Lewis coughed very silently into the crook of his arm, and
then stayed completely still. The bulldog of a man hustled
into the alley and began lifting trash-can lids, peering into
corners and kicking stacks of cardboard. He pounced on
a pile of crates, then rattled a few windows to see if they
opened. "You can't jes' disappear!" he growled into a drain-
pipe.

Sure you can, thought Lewis. If a bulldog was too stupid to
look up.

The bulldog began tipping the trash cans upside down,
then shaking each crate and cardboard bundle, being very
thorough. Lewis grew bored, then cold. The bulldog wasn't
proving nearly as entertaining as the scene at the grocery. He

wished there was another way out; Duck could have scaled the entire fire escape, sack in tow, and disappeared across the rooftops.

Below, it had gone silent; the bulldog had stopped throwing things. Lewis peered down through the metal slats. The man stood with his head cocked, like he was listening. "Hey, kid," he called abruptly. "Come on out."

Lewis frowned. The tingle returned to the base of his neck, but he told himself it was a coincidence. The bulldog could be looking for any kid.

Then, louder: "I'll give you a quarter fer what's in your pockets."

Lewis nearly toppled from his perch. What was in his pockets was his Recipe.

His felt his heart start to race. For four months the mayor, the coppers, the newspapers—heck, the entire city of Pittsburgh—attributed the Flash to a group of hardened criminals. How could this dimwit possibly know about the Recipe?

But before he had time to consider any of it, the bulldog went storming out of the alley.

Lewis quickly stood and stretched on his tiptoes. He couldn't reach the next ladder and fell against the curtained window as he tried. An old lady yanked the curtain aside and knocked the glass, crying to someone in the room, "Ernie, call the cops! It's a burglar!" Lewis scrambled back down the fire escape so fast, he left his sack of loot.

The bulldog was still in the street, so Lewis held at the edge of the alley, watching the bulldog loop back and forth along the block, checking under stoops, and asking the few passersby if they'd seen a skinny boy with brown hair. This was the Depression, there was nothing *but* skinny kids, and so the bulldog didn't get any good answers. He scowled and kicked a lamppost, and finally stalked away.

Lewis took the chance and hopped out and hustled across

the avenue, keeping his eye on the bulldog and plotting to retrieve his sack. He wanted it back. It was a waste of a day if not. Besides, those were groceries stolen by the Flash Gang. If the old lady fingered him, if—

There was a squeal of brakes, a violent honking of a car horn. Lewis turned just as a swanky black Packard came skidding around the corner. He went tumbling over one edge of its fender as it screeched to a halt.

There was an awful shout, then thudding footsteps. "*You!*"

The bulldog! Lewis could no longer pretend to not be worried. He staggered upright and took off. Behind him came a thunk and a curse as the bulldog ran smack into the auto as it started forward again. There were more honks and yells. Lewis ran as fast as he could. Behind him, the bulldog's footsteps picked up.

Go! Go! Go! Lewis raced up Penn. His lungs wouldn't last at this pace, so he made a quick calculation and peeled right onto Seventeenth Street, doubling back to St. Patrick's.

The bulldog thumped behind, flat-footed and heavy, but gaining. *Faster!* Lewis dodged bits of tin and burnt cardboard, remnants of the shantytown that once crowded near the church. Gasping, he flung himself toward the wide stone steps and stumbled up the first few before dropping to his hands and knees. His chest was seizing and breaths weren't coming.

"Wait a sec, kid!" The man stopped at the base of the steps and Lewis finally looked at him. "Let's talk!" he said, an untrustworthy grin creeping across his face.

"Got...nothing...to say," Lewis wheezed, managing another step.

"Jes' listen then. I wanna make a deal. There's twenty dollars in it for you."

Lewis froze. Twenty whole dollars...that was a fortune! He could buy food, a warmer jacket—he wouldn't need to set his Flash for a very long time. But making any sort of deal with this shady-looking character was not a good idea.

"Yeah?" Lewis panted, trying desperately to catch his breath. "Last time…you only offered…a quarter."

The bulldog was standing under a streetlamp. His gold buttons glittered in the light. So did his gold tooth as he smiled. "Aw, right. So I did. The quarter's for what's in yer pockets, kid. The twenty is for the rest of it."

The rest. Lewis knew now he was in real trouble. Somehow, the bulldog guessed not only about the Recipe in his pockets, but that Lewis kept a stash of it somewhere.

Lewis did have a stash of the Flash Recipe. It was his survival. More importantly, it was his father's. He wasn't giving that over for twenty dollars or a hundred.

With his last reserve of energy, Lewis bolted. Straight up the remaining steps, straight for the door, pulling at the iron latch. He was breathless and shaking, but still the door should have opened. The church was never locked. Lewis yanked again. And again.

A sinister little snicker sounded from below. Lewis threw himself at one of the great columns fronting the church and hauled himself up its base. He shouted down, ignoring the shaky sound of his own voice, "Don't know what you're talking about, mister."

"Yeah, you do." The bulldog's words were a whisper now. "Them ingredients you got, Lewis."

Lewis. Lewis hugged the column harder as another shock jolted through him. How in the world did this person know his name?

The bulldog began climbing the church steps slowly, like he had all the time in the world. "See," he said, "the way I figger it, you been foolin' with dangerous stuff, and havin' some grand fun." Step. "I could turn you in, tell them coppers 'bout you being the Flash Gang." Step. "I'd probably get a reward." Step. "But I don't want to do that, Lewis. I want us to be friends."

Lewis wished there was a copper around, anyone—because the only other option for escape was one Lewis hated to waste. But if this bulldog wanted the Flash, then he was going to get it.

Lewis jammed his hand into his left pocket, pulled out the pouch, trying to turn it inside out so he could smear the remaining sludge on the towering column in front of him.

"No, you don't!" More nimbly than seemed possible, the bulldog leaped the last steps and grabbed him by the jacket. Lewis twisted, kicking, but something soft and sickly sweet got shoved under his nose and made him go limp. The bulldog snagged the little pouch from his hand and then tucked Lewis under his arm like a suitcase and clunked back down the steps of St. Patrick's.

The last thought Lewis had before dropping into blackness was that it was too bad nobody would notice.

3

KIDNAPPED

What a bumpy trolley, Lewis thought groggily. His stomach was flip-flopping worse than a jumping bean.

He should get off. It wasn't worth the nickel to feel sick. But when Lewis reached for the bell cord, there was nothing there. He tried standing up, but his feet couldn't get any purchase. Was he even sitting down?

Lewis forced one eyelid open, then the other. *Impossible.* He nudged his eyeglasses into place and looked again—no, the sidewalk was indeed swinging alarmingly close to his nose.

He wasn't on a trolley at all but hanging over a beefy, green-sleeved arm.

I'm being kidnapped by a bulldog in a green suit. That sounded ridiculous, even to Lewis. But there he was, upside down, with no idea how he'd got there. His brain felt like it was underwater with only bits of memory sticking out—something about twenty dollars and the steps of St. Patrick's.

The bulldog wheeled abruptly and mounted some steps. There was the pounding of a fist, then the scraping of a heavy door opening, and an abrupt rise in temperature. They were going indoors. And then, as Lewis was hauled over the doorjamb, he began to hear (or was it dream?) a conversation.

"What is *that*? What are you doing? Why did you bring him here?"

"Oh, be quiet. I had to imper'vise."

"Not here! Improvise somewhere else!"

The voice was definitely a lady's. A hoity-sounding crust of a lady. And she was filled with fury, though the green bulldog didn't seem to care. He simply lugged Lewis along under the shower of chastising and dumped him—on a sofa, Lewis thought vaguely. The pit of his stomach went flying dizzily to his head.

The lady spluttered, "Not upstairs! Anyone could see!" A pair of bony fingers grabbed at Lewis's shoulders, but the bulldog's rough, calloused hands brusquely intervened and dragged Lewis up.

"All right, all right. Whatcha want me ta do with him, then?"

"Oh, honestly. This way."

And they were off again, this time led by the angry lady— and followed, Lewis suddenly thought, by a smaller, more fluttery someone. There were soft, light footsteps by his right ear.

The fluttery someone drew the lady's wrath. She screeched, "Go back upstairs this instant, missy!"

The soft footsteps faded, and Lewis was bumped through a doorway and down a set of stairs. Each thunk brushed away a little of the fuzziness, so Lewis thought he should count, to try and orient himself. *Eight steps going down. Six straight on.*

They stopped. There was a rustle, then a jingling of keys. The lady was sorting through a ring of them, and *humph*ing in a most perturbed way. "Explain exactly why you brought that filthy urchin here."

She fitted a key into a lock. *Door*, Lewis noted, though that seemed too obvious to count.

"Well, we can't bring him to the boss till we know he's the right kid," said the bulldog.

The fiddling stopped. "You don't know? You buffoon! How dare you waste my time!"

"Aw stuff it, would ya?"

"This is my home, Mr. Scrugg, not a way station!" The locked door banged open.

"Sure, Tildy," said Mr. Scrugg easily.

Mr. Scrugg. Tildy. Lewis was hiked forward and plunked into a seat. *Musty room. Wooden chair. Four steps from the door.* Lewis let his head droop. His brain was working faster now, organizing an escape. He would stay limp, pretending he was asleep, then run at the first moment of distraction. The odd pair were still arguing, which was a very good distraction, but they were saying lots of curious things that caught Lewis's attention.

"This is terrible. You're a stupid oaf."

"What was I supposed to do? The kid's stubborn."

"He's a child, Mr. Scrugg! Make him do whatever you want."

There was a sudden thud overhead and then a giant scraping sound, as if something were being dragged along the floor above them.

Scrugg snorted. "Yeah, because you have a real way with children, Tildy."

When the lady spoke again, it was squeezed and vicious sounding. "If the boy is unfortunately here, where are the materials? You did get them, didn't you?"

Scrugg growled, "Like I said, I had to imper'vise. He's got some of the stuff on 'im. I got one, here's the other."

Mr. Scrugg took the pouch from Lewis's right pocket. Lewis grit his teeth, held very, very still. He remembered now: Scrugg wanted his Recipe stash.

"That's them? Oh, you imbecile! You'll blow up my house!"

"Relax, will ya? It's jes' two ingredients. Boy's only got two. Didn't the boss say it takes all three?"

Lewis heard Scrugg stomp away.

"Where are you going?" The lady's footsteps were nervous-sounding, click-clicking after the bulldog. Lewis risked a quick glance, but his glasses were dangling from one ear and he couldn't see.

"I'm bringing these to the shop," said Scrugg. "The Deutscher's gotta test it."

"You're leaving?" The lady was beside herself. "What if the boy wakes up and starts banging on the door? What if he screams? I have neighbors, you know!"

Scrugg stomped back toward Lewis and Lewis shut his eyes tight. There was a rustling sound, the creak of Scrugg's heavy feet. A moment later Lewis's hands were abruptly yanked behind his back and tied with a very stiff rope.

And then, so were his ankles.

Lewis's heart began thudding. He opened his mouth to cry out but a grubby handkerchief that tasted of oil and stank of sweat was forced between his teeth and knotted at the back of his neck. The bulldog patted the top of Lewis's head and, with a snort, straightened Lewis's eyeglasses.

"Satisfied, Tildy?"

Scrugg thudded away as Lewis jerked his head up, eyes wide. He couldn't stay like this! He had the barest moment to see that he was in a windowless room before the bulldog flicked a light switch and shut the door, plunging Lewis into pitch black.

"Mmmmnf!" he cried after them.

The kidnappers didn't hear or care; they were quarreling in the hallway, their voices muffled by the door.

"Children like this…bad enough in the street, but my home!" the lady spat in disgust. "How long am I supposed to monitor this…this boy?"

"Stop whinin'. Once we know fer sure it's him, the Flash Gang boy, we'll go forward with the plan. Meantime, the Deutscher can work with what's in his pockets. Jes' keep cool fer now, and—"

Then there was a sudden and tremendous crash from above, as if something very large had shattered, followed by the sound of footsteps scuttling across the ceiling. The Tildy woman made a strangled hiss.

Mr. Scrugg finished his sentence: "—and fer chrissake, mind after your real problems till I get back."

The two retreated quickly in clicks and clomps, down the hall and up the eight stairs. There was a heavy slam of a door followed by muffled yelling from Tildy. And then those noises, too, faded.

Lewis's breath came in awkward little pants. He curled his fingers to his binds. If he could just get his thumb under the loop, a fingernail to pry the knots loose…But his thumb couldn't reach, his nails were too short, and the drugs made his hands feel thick and clumsy. His fingers scrabbled over the impossibly tight knots, while dread fizzed into his lungs—they would squeeze completely shut if he panicked.

Lewis clenched his jaw. *Focus!* he told himself sternly. *Room. Chair. Steps. Rope. Room. Chair. Steps. Rope.* He repeated the words, reminding himself of what his dad would say: that panic was just his brain having a tantrum and to take three very slow breaths instead. So he did, paying close attention to his lungs expanding and releasing.

Slowly, the fizzing subsided. But it was awful—being trapped in the pitch dark, and not knowing for how long he might be kept there. Lewis forced himself to stay focused, first on his lungs inflating, and then on small things, like not tasting the handkerchief and flexing his wrists so his fingers didn't tingle. Bigger thoughts, however, couldn't help but creep in. Lewis wondered how Scrugg had found him. What did he want the Recipe for anyway? And what did he mean by "three" ingredients? Lewis's Recipe was just two ingredients, the ash and the sludge, and he was the only one who knew anything about them.

Lewis had discovered the Flash by accident. Its ingredients were results of a recycling project his father, a chemistry professor, had been working on. They'd been stored under the kitchen sink in two heavy brass pots, with a Do Not Touch sign on them. His father was absentminded about most things, but not about his pots. "Mind the pots," he'd say to Lewis each time he went out. And then one time he went out and didn't come back.

But Lewis had minded the pots, minded them enough to rescue them when the nasty landlady kicked him out. Lewis had snuck back and retrieved a change of clothes, a spoon, a cup, and the pots, which he'd stowed behind some shrubs in the garden and transported later with a borrowed hand truck. He was proud of rescuing his dad's pots. It was only later, after Lewis was struggling on his own, that he broke the Do Not Touch rule. That's when he found that if the pots' contents were mixed in the right proportion, an amazing flash of light resulted. The ingredients had saved him.

Now he had to save the ingredients from Scrugg. Lewis felt a burn of indignation, realizing that he was going to have to wait for the bulldog to return and untie him before he could do so.

But the bulldog didn't return. Neither did the crust lady or anyone else. There were no more thuds, or voices. Lewis tried marking the minutes, certain that one hour, then two had passed, then three. The house was eerily quiet and the quiet made it harder for Lewis to keep track—of the time, of an escape plan, of how many meals he was missing. His thoughts wandered back to his dad and he pictured his father's eyes crinkling behind the tortoiseshell glasses that were just like Lewis's own. He pictured their upstairs rooms and the lampshades his dad had fashioned with wire hangers and brown paper bags, and how they made the room golden warm with their light. He missed that light, caught as he was in the dark. He missed his dad. He tried picturing more things from home, like supper and pillows, but the stupid basement doorknob was jiggling and ruining every—

Doorknob?

Lewis jerked awake, unaware he'd fallen asleep, *furious* he'd fallen asleep. The kidnappers were back and he wasn't prepared! He didn't have time to remember any plan. He couldn't even—

The door flung open.

There was a sharp pause and a great intake of breath. Lewis braced for the bulldog or the snake. But, instead of a gravelly rasp or angry snip, it was an angelic and dramatic voice that exclaimed:

"It is I, Pearl Alice Clavell! And I have come to save you!"

4

THE WORST RESCUE EVER

Lights flashed on. Lewis squinted. At first, he wasn't quite sure what, exactly, had come. It was a blurry froth of bows and curls—like an enormous, frilly birthday cake.

Then his eyes adjusted and Lewis saw a girl about his age wearing the pinkest of ballerina tutus: layers and layers of gauze for the skirt and rose appliqués along the neckline. She had on a pink sweater and pink stockings and pink ballet slippers and a huge pink ribbon tying perfect blond ringlets. She had perfect features, too, like one of those china dolls, or glamorous stars in the movie magazines—with big blue eyes, fluttery eyelashes, and a bow-shaped mouth. She also gripped a butter knife in one hand with such ferocity he wasn't quite sure if he was supposed to be relieved or scared. But regardless, if this Pearl Alice Clavell intended to rescue him, Lewis figured she ought to get on with it.

"Mmmmnf!" Lewis shouted as best he could.

"Yes, Sir Nigel!" she replied. "Hope is restored!" While Lewis watched, dumbfounded, the girl took three steps back, closed her eyes, took a deep breath, then made a very awkward pirouette and leap, and landed about two feet from Lewis. She muttered something under her breath, backed up and started her twirl and jump over again. This time Pearl Alice Clavell landed at Lewis's feet and she beamed victoriously.

"'Tragic Trapeze,'" she announced, as if that explained anything. Then she took the butter knife in both hands and began sawing at the binds on his ankles.

"Mmnf! Mmnf!" Lewis begged. Pearl was wholly fixed on

her task. "Mmnf!" It was only when he tried kicking her that she thought to remove his gag.

Lewis spit out as much of the taste of the handkerchief as he could. "That knife won't work," he panted.

"Yes, it will. I have spent *months* planning this," Pearl assured him. She attacked the knots again.

"How about you just untie me?" Lewis asked. "That'd be a whole lot quicker."

"Have no fear. I am an expert at escape. This is the best way."

A long moment of sawing later, Lewis tried again (as patiently as he could muster given the circumstances). "Could you do me a favor, considering I'm the one all knotted? Take the end of the rope just by my thumb and push it up and to the right. The rope's stiff enough, it'll slide through easy."

Pearl paused in her sawing, studied him for a moment. Then she put her hand on her heart and turned her enormous blue eyes skyward. "For you," she declared with a tremendous sigh, and hung in that pose.

This had to be the worst rescue ever. But just as Lewis was furiously considering his next option, Pearl righted herself, whisked behind the chair and did as he'd asked, and of course the rope slid apart just as he'd said. She went for the knots at his feet again, but Lewis nudged her away. "Thanks. I'll do it."

In a moment, Lewis was free. He pushed from the chair and crashed immediately to the floor from being so stiff.

"You poor thing! Your legs have fallen asleep!" Pearl flung herself next to him and began prodding violently at his legs. "Fear not, I am an expert at acupuncture."

"Stop poking me please. And I'm not afra—Ow! Wait! Just…" Lewis managed to squirm out from under her, then scrabbled to the door, and limped down the hall as fast as he could. He could see it all now—the narrow hallway, and the wooden stairs just ahead. *Six steps, eight…* he counted, trying to ignore the burning feeling in his lungs. Luckily the girl had gone back for her butter knife, which gave Lewis a head start, but a moment later he heard, "Wait! Where are you going?" and was abruptly tackled halfway up the stairs. "You're supposed to follow me!" Pearl insisted as they slid all the way back to the bottom.

"Ouch!" yelped Lewis, trying to claw his way out from under all the tulle. "I've got to get out of here! Let go!"

"I'm saving you!" She hugged him tighter. "You can't do this without me!"

"Thank you for untying me, but now get off!"

"But I'm a prisoner too!" she said with desperation.

"You don't look like one!"

"I am!" Lewis had wriggled mostly out of her grasp, but the girl still clung to his ankles. "I am a *famous* heiress," she whispered, as if betraying a deepest secret. "And Aunt Gimlick is a spy and very jealous of me. She locks the doors, and I'm *forced* to be her slave."

Louis stopped struggling. "The lady who lives here is your aunt? What are you helping me for?"

"I—" Pearl abruptly stopped and took a deep breath. For a moment Lewis thought she might answer honestly, but then her eyes slid heavenward again and her voice went so tremulous it made her whole body vibrate. "I have been waiting *ever* so long for my chance, and here you are! We can save the world now, Nigel."

"Look, I'm not…" Lewis gave up. Famous heiress, nonsense-spouter, and whatever acupuncture was…he had no idea what to make of Pearl Alice Clavell, but he couldn't waste any time trying to figure it out. "Where's your aunt?" he asked urgently.

"Oh, our jailor is far, far away. We have *hours* to escape. I have planned this perfectly." Pearl scrambled up the stairs ahead of him. "This way!" she whispered loudly, as if there were another option. She took her knife in her right hand, cracked open the basement door with her left, and waited for Lewis to reach the step just beneath hers. "The coast is clear!" she announced, then swung the door wide.

It was a spare and spotless hallway foyer. A wide staircase swept down before them, topped with a highly polished banister. Beside the staircase ran a small corridor that led to a sitting room, and on the opposite side of this room was a large front door with a glass transom. Just seeing the hazy daylight was deliriously thrilling. But no sooner had Lewis stepped out of the basement than he stopped dead. Agitated click-clicking footsteps sounded just overhead and a crusty voice shrieked, "Pearl!"

"You said she was far away!" gasped Lewis.

The aunt wasn't far away. In fact, she was on the second-floor landing, peering down at them—a tall, ramrod-straight lady in a red-and-white pinstripe dress, with a topping of vivid strawberry-red hair, and, apparently, steam spewing from her ears. "What are you doing?"

"Run!" Pearl screamed. She didn't need to because Lewis was already running. Away from the stairs and, unfortunately, the front door.

"Stop this instant!" Aunt Gimlick charged for the staircase, but her heel caught on the stair runner, and she went careening down the stairs feet first, screeching with each bump: "Don't. You. Dare. Move. An. Inch!" She landed in a sprawl at the bottom, writhing like an enormous peppermint snake.

Lewis found himself in a parlor, a dead end. He doubled back for the front door, trying to hop over the lady. She caught him by a shoelace. "You. Stay!"

"This way!" Pearl was madly signaling.

Lewis yanked his foot free and tore after Pearl, who'd hiked left down a hallway. "Some rescue!" he panted.

"Stop!" Aunt Gimlick thundered from behind. She'd gotten to her feet and was storming after them.

"Hurry!" Pearl picked up the pace. "In here!"

Lewis followed, hurtling through a dining room and into a large, cold-looking kitchen. "How do you get out of here?"

Pearl planted herself in front of the door they'd just barreled through, her arms spread wide. "There!" she cried, pointing behind her. "I'll hold her off!"

Lewis flung himself through a swinging door at the back of the kitchen and found himself in a pantry, an immaculate and very long corridor with shelves of things all neatly stacked and labeled. There was a back door at its end. Lewis didn't even try to collect his breath, he just ran. Behind him there was a slam, a thud, a screech, and then Aunt Gimlick's voice, huge with fury, screaming, "What have you done? You'll ruin everything!"

"Kidnapper! Traitor! Fascist! Spy!" cried Pearl.

"This is the last straw, young lady! I will string you up by your ears!"

Lewis heard a shuffle and a yelp from Pearl that sounded as if her arm was being twisted. And though he had his hand on the doorknob and was just a step away from freedom, he turned around, grabbed the first thing he could get his hands on, which happened to be a canister of flour, and plowed back into the kitchen.

Aunt Gimlick was not twisting Pearl's arm. Rather, Pearl clung to her aunt's back, and her aunt was lurching about the kitchen trying to claw her off. She'd grabbed a great handful of Pearl's curls and yanked as the girl shouted.

Lewis pried the top off the canister. "Hey!" he called to the snake. "Catch!"

If you tell people to catch, he knew, they almost instinctively try. Aunt Gimlick did. Her hands reflexively went up, leaving Pearl to tumble sideways. One moment the canister was flying through the air, and the next a cloud of flour enveloped all of them. Lewis turned and ran.

The aunt began shrieking; Pearl was on her feet, running

faster than Lewis—through the pantry, out the back door, through the little gate that opened to a driveway. They kept running for two more blocks before Lewis staggered behind a clump of garbage cans and began hacking for breath.

Pearl stopped too. She waited, watching in such a curious and eager way as he coughed and spat out stringy things that Lewis felt fiercely embarrassed. And then when he'd finally quieted, she pulled her gauzy skirts wide and sank into a curtsy. Something like a curtsy anyway—she fell over while doing it. Flour drifted from her curls.

"*My* Nigel," she sighed, and put her hand over her heart.

Lewis cleared his throat. There was flour up his nose and it made his lungs hurt worse. And now this very odd girl was folded over in front of him blocking his exit. And she'd given him a terrible name.

"Lewis," he corrected stiffly. "My name is Lewis."

Then, while she was still in her curtsy, Lewis maneuvered around her, struggled across the street and turned the corner, eager to disappear into the gloom of Pittsburgh.

5

THE EXPERT AT EVERYTHING

Lewis walked blindly in one direction then another. His chest ached; each breath burned. *Focus*, he told himself, but on what? The surroundings were bland and colorless in the ever-present sooty haze. There were square houses all the same size, each fronted by the same square porch. He didn't know the neighborhood; he didn't know how far he was from the abandoned factory where he slept. He didn't even know what day it was.

Still, Pittsburgh was unique with its steep ridges. Lewis figured, after a block or two and some easier breaths, that he might be on top of one of those ridges, judging from the way the smog drifted low, leaving the gray afternoon sky above just a tiny bit paler…rather like the manner in which the cloud of flour had surrounded that peppermint snake.

Good riddance, snake. He might be slightly lost, but at least the ordeal with that lady and her curious niece was over.

Except, not quite. For suddenly he heard: "That was 'Thundering Thieves' and 'Sunset Sabotage' all rolled into one!"

Pearl Alice Clavell emerged from the soot and landed on the sidewalk behind Lewis in a shower of pink tulle.

"You were absolutely *brilliant* with the flour, Nigel!" she said, fluffing her skirt. "Aunt Gimlick cannot *abide* messes. And my judo expertise completely overwhelmed her, just as I planned."

Lewis stood gaping. "You—you followed me? Why did you follow me?"

Pearl didn't seem to hear. Her eyes were closed and she

was busy reenacting the encounter with her aunt by wrapping her arms around her ears. "I had her trapped in my headlock. My headlock is famous, you know."

An hour ago, you were a famous heiress, Lewis thought, but snapped his mouth shut before saying it aloud. He had no intention of encouraging her. This girl couldn't carry on a logical conversation, and she was clearly not the sort to let people go their own way and mind their own business. Raising his collar against the chill, he turned sharply and began walking away.

"My hands are deadly weapons," Pearl added from behind.

Just swell. Glancing back, Lewis bit his tongue against the fierce retort that rose in his throat. Pearl's china-doll face lit up.

"I'm not looking at you!" he insisted. "I'm checking to see who else is chasing me!"

That was the important thing—that those grown-ups weren't there. He was pretty sure Aunt Gimlick hadn't followed him, but maybe at this very instant she was calling the odious Mr. Scrugg and he was on his way, with his sickly sweet cloths and calloused hands and stolen Recipe pouches—

"Oh, not to worry." Pearl blithely interrupted what very much were worries. "I have excellent instincts. We are safe."

We? Lewis felt his cheeks grow hot. He shouldn't have gone back to help this girl. He'd given her the wrong idea, obviously, and now she was making it hard to disappear. And Lewis needed to disappear. Give him a minute and he'd figure out where he was, and then he could vanish just fine into the sooty fog. But she, this Pearl Alice Clavell, was impossible to miss in that get-up. The pink glowed like starshine, for Pete's sake.

"There is no 'we,'" Lewis stated emphatically. "We don't know each other. Let's keep it that way!" He pointed behind Pearl, a clear indication that she was to turn back. When she didn't take the hint, he wheeled sharply once more and marched around one corner and another, increasing his pace as best he could; then he spied a landmark.

Herron Hill Park was to his right, the entrance crowded with hobos and un-watched children playing jacks and hopscotch. On the stone-bordered steps that led to the flat and treeless courtyard someone had marked the ground with a wide, squared U, which he knew was hobo code for "Camp Here." Someone else had scrawled, "Give me a job!" That was scratched over with a large Nazi swastika. Pearl stopped to look, but Lewis refused to think about any of it. He hustled past the hobos and the children, then up a slope and back to the street. He headed north with his quickest stride.

But his stride hadn't been quick enough.

Pearl Alice Clavell easily fell into line with him, her blond ringlets bouncing under the perfect pink ribbon. "So," she asked, "where are we going?"

"What?" yelped Lewis.

"Do you live near here?" she continued. "That gray house back there was nice. I've pictured you having a library, Nigel. And a tiger—do you have a pet tiger? You should wear an ascot and tuck a pipe in your vest pocket. Have you been expelled from school too? I can't wait to meet your parents—I make the most wonderful daughter."

Lewis pressed his lips together. Was she really this loopy? Nobody could be this loopy! He had to stop this immediately.

Lewis whirled to face her. "Hey, are you hungry?"

Pearl's expression immediately went from dreamy to pathetic. "Oh yes, Nigel! Aren't we *ever* so desperate?" She staggered a bit as proof. "Perhaps we can scrounge the tiniest morsel of food to stave off those eager vultures." She pointed at a disinterested crow sitting atop a lamppost.

"Yeah, uh, okay." Lewis bit back the laugh that nearly burst out. "This way then."

And he proceeded to lead Pearl Alice Clavell through

the sadder Pittsburgh, over uneven pavers, along decrepit streets, down two rickety staircases, and across one narrow footbridge. Lewis expected—hoped, at least—she would drop away, the way a dog starts to follow and then gives up when you leave its territory. But Pearl did not. Nor did she complain about the route or the sharpening cold of the late March afternoon. She padded along in her thin ballet slippers, enthusiastically narrating their trek with warnings of quicksand, vines, and leeches, as if they were machete-ing their way through the darkest jungle.

When Lewis finally stopped, they were across from the stinking and distinctly non-jungle Allegheny River, which glugged along, steel gray and icy cold. In front of the river loomed North Market, an enormous and crowded warehouse where farmers, butchers, and anyone trying to make a penny came to sell their wares. It was the perfect place to ditch someone.

"Civilization!" Pearl cried behind him. "We are *saved*! This is a cavern of *feasts*—a corn-u-COPia…!"

Lewis marched across the cobbles straight into the market's truck-sized entrance. Earthy, rotting vegetable smells blended with sweet scents of pastry and the cloying stench of meat. A pang of hunger stabbed his belly.

Shaking himself, he looked about for a good ditching spot, then navigated to the busiest section. He pointed at the first thing he saw: some overripe, speckled bananas.

"Wow! Would you look at those!" he exclaimed loudly. "The rarest of rare! All the way from…from…Timbuktu!"

"Papa ate bananas in Timbuktu!" Pearl gasped with delight and turned to look. When she did, Lewis dove between a poultry and a pig stall and crawled away as fast as he could. "Nigel? Sir Nigel?" went lilting above the din behind him.

So long, Pearl Clavell, Lewis snickered. He would suffer no partners, especially one who talked so much and had kidnappers for relatives. And if there were any twinges of guilt, he'd ignore them. He wouldn't want to live with that wretched aunt either, but that didn't make this girl his problem to solve.

A few aisles later, hands and knees in a mix of sawdust, feathers, and some other things he preferred not to identify, Lewis scrambled up—maintaining a crouch—and hustled off to the side entrance.

Very soon he was sorry that he'd chosen North Market as the ditching place. The route was a gauntlet of temptation—meat pies, corned beef sandwiches, sugared doughnuts…even pickles—all begging to be eaten while also being completely un-pinchable, with the vendors keeping a sharp lookout for streeters. And who was he kidding anyway? He wasn't quick-fingered. He needed the Flash for distraction and Scrugg had taken his pouches. He'd have to replenish his supply.

A hot stab of anger flushed his cheeks. Could he even use his Recipe again? Would the bulldog be watching for him—for the Flash Gang? It was so unfair, this kidnapping business. Lewis scowled as he imagined living off his supply of tinned food, which seemed terribly meager given the depths of his hunger.

Worse, as Lewis scooted out of the market, he was waylaid by the most enchanting smell. A cluster of people surrounded a cart where a man was crisping slices of freshly peeled potatoes and trading a sleeve of them for a nickel. The scent was salty and greasy and potato-y. Lewis froze with longing.

No Flash, no chips. But the peels were another matter. They were discards, in a slimy mound on the asphalt by the man's feet. Potato peels weren't bad when they were crisped in a frying pan with lard and salt, though crisping one at a time by candle flame with no salt wasn't quite the same.

Still, peels it was.

Lewis stepped forward, reaching out a hand, but a grimy woman appeared from nowhere, knocking him back with her foot. "Them's spoken fer!" she barked.

"It's just a handful!" he protested, to which she snapped, "I got four boys punier 'n you!"

At that, the vendor turned and swatted them both with a handy broom, shouting, "Beat it, you trash!" There was a sudden chaos of stick and bristles, splatters of hot oil, and the woman's curses ringing in Lewis's ears. He ducked under the flying broom and pushed himself as fast as he could up Smallman Street. He didn't stop until he hit the railroad tracks, and when he did stop he plopped down, wheezing and humiliated. And still hungry. And now night was closing in, the air turning thick with a threat of snow.

He hugged his legs and dropped his head to his knees. He hated feeling sorry for himself. Other people suffered worse than he did—like that potato-peel lady with her puny boys. Still, how miserable these past days had been!

At length, Lewis got up. He was free. That was enough for now. And he did have enough tinned food at the factory to see him through the next couple of meals and plenty of Recipe to get fresh food later; he'd just have to be extra-specially clever about not being seen after setting it off. He brushed the remaining sawdust off his hands and knees, then hiked over the tracks toward his shelter.

Between Smallman Street and the Allegheny River was a weed-trampled lot, crisscrossed with abandoned railroad tracks. An eight-foot-tall chain-link fence bordered one end, and inside the fence sat a hollow factory. It was brick, with a single smokestack and big, empty banks of windows facing the river. Painted letters under the windows spelled out GRUB FITTINGS & SPECIAL... The rest of the sign had long since been worn off.

Lewis crossed the lot to the fence, then walked along the fence to the edge of the river. He skidded a few feet down the riverbank to where the mouth of a large drain tunnel jutted from the dirt. The tunnel had once spewed waste from the factory directly into the river far below. Now it was dry, its opening closed up with a large cement block. The block was not as heavy as it looked. Lewis had put it there to keep trespassers from doing what he'd done: crawl through the tunnel straight into the pits of the Grub factory.

The factory was Lewis's makeshift residence. For nearly four months he'd been its only inhabitant, which was exactly how he wanted it. The factory was decrepit and spare, but safe. And tonight, after everything that had happened, it felt almost better than makeshift. He reached for the block.

"Sir Nigel!"

Lewis felt his feet freeze and his cheeks blaze. He poked his head above the bank. *Impossible.* There, coming across the tracks straight for him, was that beacon of pink tulle and bouncy curls.

"You were marvelous fending off that evil chef and his broom!" Pearl leaped over a section of track, shook her head, doubled back, and tried the leap again, whispering what sounded like "Tragic Trapeze" again under her breath. Aloud she said, "And how clever to find this darkest of trysting places to reunite!"

Lewis watched, glued to his spot, as she skipped right to him and dropped into that dreadfully awkward curtsy.

"For you, my liege." Then she reached down and opened her hand to reveal the crumbs of what had been potato chips.

"How—?" Lewis spluttered, turning even redder. It was too incredible. He refused the chips on principle.

Pearl straightened and popped the crumbs in her mouth, looking very pleased.

"In 'Beggar's Burial,'" she chomped, "Lola Lavender and Sir Nigel survived on chips for three weeks in that abandoned mine."

"Lola LAVENDER?" Lewis shouted, his frustration propelling his voice straight across the barren lot. "You're imitating LOLA LAVENDER? You're bonkers!" *The Adventures of Lola Lavender* was a weekly radio show about a young heiress on a zillion escapades, usually accompanied by her wimpy sidekick, Sir Nigel Davenport.

Enough was enough. Lewis dug his fingers into the dirt and scrambled up the bank to meet Pearl Alice Clavell eye to eye. He put his hands on his hips to make himself bigger and said firmly, "Look here. This isn't some radio adventure! It's cold out and dark and your aunt helped kidnap me and I—I've had enough! You were nice to offer the chips; now go home!" He folded his arms across his chest.

Pearl licked the salt from her fingers and said, with irritating assuredness, "Papa is otherwise occupied collecting jewels on the Nile, and I can no longer be a party to the treasonous activities of my dreadful aunt. I'd been waiting for my chance and then you arrived! So, while I work to thwart her, my home is with you."

"What? No, it's not." Lewis pushed past her and stomped across the lot, thinking he needed somehow to lead Pearl away from the factory and his stash of Recipe. Pearl followed right behind.

"Well, I rescued you!" she countered.

"Are you kidding? I tossed the flour. I saved *you*!" Lewis flung over his shoulder. He hadn't a clue where to go. He hadn't a clue why Pearl didn't seem to be tired.

"Oh pooh," she said. "You owe me. You have—"

She never finished. The world seemed to explode just then, with one great crash of sound followed by a shock wave that knocked them to the ground, where they lay side by side, stunned. Stars swirled above Lewis; his ears rang. He struggled up and looked toward the direction of the blast, toward a neighborhood, three or four blocks away.

"What was that?" Pearl gasped. Gone was her blithe tone. It was the first time Pearl Alice Clavell sounded remotely genuine, as if she had forgotten her Lola Lavender act.

A column of blue-tinged smoke was rising into the air, climbing and changing color from blue to orange to white as it flooded over the roofs of the surrounding houses. Just like an enormous, blinding umbrella of light.

"Oh! The stench! We're dying!" Pearl dramatically gripped at her neck, making ridiculous choking sounds.

So much for genuine. Lewis shook his head.

"It's straight out of 'Beyond Beirut'!" she cried.

"Oh stop!" he croaked. "It's just sulfur. The rotten-egg smell won't hurt you."

Rotten eggs. Dread washed over Lewis. *No. No. It couldn't be—could it?*

"Rotten…what? Wait. Wait!" Pearl rolled across the ground to Lewis and clutched at his arm. "Nigel! Do you realize what that is? It's the Flash Gang! The actual Flash Gang! Maybe we can see them!" Pearl pried a splintered piece of track from the frozen ground. Holding it in front of her like a sword, she scrambled to her feet and charged across the vacant lot.

Lewis didn't move. He stared at the umbrella of light. "It's not the Flash Gang!" he yelled after her, and then, more quietly, as if to convince himself, "It's not!" But his heart was pounding.

"Don't you read the papers?" she called back. "They're the most notorious gang in Pittsburgh! Financed by Fat Joe and the mob! They strike with some sort of fantastical weapon that *blinds* you and leaves a *blue* mark and *smells like rotten eggs!*"

Just then, careening along Smallman Street came two police cars, then a fire truck and then…And then the Buick from the *Post-Gazette*.

Pearl, poised at the edge of the street, called back to Lewis, "Come on, Nigel! We have to see this!"

And Lewis, despite the perfect opportunity to slip away while Pearl wasn't paying attention, only said, "I'm coming."

6

A STINK

"This way, Nigel!" cried Pearl, racing down the street. At a block of row houses she came to a halt and pointed at one. "There," she exclaimed.

Lewis followed by rote, crossing where Pearl crossed and turning where Pearl turned. He didn't even care about being called Nigel. His mind was fiercely trying to explain what had just happened. The explosion couldn't have had anything to do with the Flash. Of course not. His Recipe couldn't produce such a massive *boom*, or that column of blue turning to orange and then white.

But with every footfall one word kept pounding in his head: *Scrugg, Scrugg, Scrugg,* so that when Lewis turned the corner onto Butler Street, there was a single thought, like an ugly chill, curling through him: *What had the bulldog done with his Recipe?*

Pearl stopped. They were at the block where the explosion had taken place. It was packed with dozens of onlookers spilling over the sidewalk and pouring into the street, in shirtsleeves and aprons, interrupted from dinner, having raced outside without their overcoats. His dad would have done the same thing, Lewis noted faintly. He would have dashed outside, unsuitably dressed for winter, ever absent-minded, ever curious.

A large fire engine parted the throng with great blasts of its horn and then screeched to a halt. Headlights from two police vehicles lit up the firemen, who climbed on top of their truck and readied ladders and hoses. The reporter in the trilby was weaving back and forth, taking statements from anyone who'd talk. The air was thick with the stink of sulfur, and everyone stood on their toes to squint through the haze, waving hands in front of their noses. Enterprising streeters were already nudging about the crowd, using the dark and the distraction to pinch loose change from people's pockets.

One streeter clung to a lamppost above the crowd, his head silhouetted in the glare of headlights. Lewis immediately recognized the narrow face with its beaky nose.

Mac was surveying the scene. He spied Lewis, and his sharp little face stretched wide in a grin.

"Brain!" he shouted, waving an arm. "We beat ya this time! Come here, this is a heck of a clamor!"

"What happened?" Lewis shouted back, squeezing through a forest of elbows.

"There's a little building over there," Mac reported when Lewis popped out at the base of the lamppost. "Its roof went right up like a roman candle!" He drew his finger up toward where the moon would be if it weren't so cloudy. "Duck and me saw it from blocks away. We never ran so fast!" Mac hopped down and socked Lewis in the arm for emphasis.

He didn't mention the Flash Gang, Lewis thought, somewhat relieved. "So what do you—"

Pearl emerged from the throng and reattached herself to Lewis, saying brightly, "Here you are!"

Lewis shrugged out of her grip and tried again. "What do you think happ—?" then gave up. Mac had frozen at Pearl's arrival, his red-splotched face turning even redder.

Pearl, in all her fluffy pink glory, dropped into that terrible half-curtsy. "Pardon me, sir." And then she went right past both of them, eyes on the lamppost. She made a completely unnecessary leap, banged into the post, then scrabbled up, dislodged Mac, and cried, "What views lie beyond?"

"Who's your friend?" Mac landed on the ground and whispered to Lewis in awe.

Lewis groaned. "She's not my"—but that was drowned out by Pearl, who looked down and saluted Mac, correcting, "*Best* friend. And savior." She lowered herself a bit and stretched out a hand. "Pearl Alice Clavell, Master Detective. And you are, sir?"

"Uh…Mac," Mac said, as if he wasn't quite sure. Gingerly, he took her hand and gave it a little shake, his blush burning right to the tips of his big ears.

Lewis rolled his eyes. "For Pete's sake. Let me up there!"

"But of course, my liege." Pearl let go of Mac and reached out to Lewis. Lewis took her hand, gritting his teeth that he needed her help to climb up. He hooked both arms and a leg around one side of the post for support. Pearl, on the other side of the post, fashioned her hands into an imaginary telescope and peered at him expectantly.

Lewis pushed away her hands and shifted so that he could see.

Wedged between a filling station and a cluttered alley was a narrow, rundown shop, its front grimy with ash and peeling paint. A torn awning hung over the door and a small Watch Repair sign was taped to the cracked front window. Firemen stood idle, holding dry hoses. There wasn't much they could do. None of the other buildings were harmed, and the shop didn't appear to be on fire, although a thin curl of smoke seeped through a hole in its roof.

Pearl gasped. "Oh my! The Mysterious Jeweler!"

"What?" Lewis whipped around, lost his balance, and slid off the lamppost, landing hard on his backside. Pearl took the opportunity to dismount, kicking one leg straight into the air and sailing out, her tutu fluttering. Amazingly (Lewis thought so anyway) she landed almost upright in front of Mac, who had been staring boggle-eyed at Pearl the entire time.

Pearl didn't acknowledge either of them. She'd already clasped her hands behind her back and was beginning to pace in a circle, looking very detective-like. "The Mysterious Jeweler," she repeated as she paced. After two circles Pearl paused, looked up, and exclaimed, "An *extraordinary* plot twist, Nigel!" Then she resumed pacing.

"Who's Nigel?" Mac asked.

"Don't ask," said Lewis and changed the subject. "Where's Duck?"

"Huh?" Mac replied blankly.

"Duck."

"Oh." Mac shook himself out of his Pearl stupor. "He's gone 'round back, seeing what's to see." Mac leaned closer to Lewis and whispered, "Watch repair, right? Means there'll be a rich haul. I said to go for some heavy pockets first, but Duck's aiming to get inside the shop. You know him. He likes stuff more than money."

Pearl had circled around to face them. She announced quite gravely, "You realize, gentlemen, that the watch repair is just a front. Evil-doing abounds behind that door."

Before Lewis could roll his eyes again, a great, barrel-chested copper called out to the crowd, "All right, folks." He spread his arms out wide. "Nothing to see here. A gas stove popped, that's all. Everybody go home now." The copper stopped just in front of Lewis, his gaze settling on the three of them—two now, since Mac had magically melted out of sight. The copper's eyes narrowed. "Now," he reiterated sternly.

Lewis's throat went dry, but Pearl leaped forward. "Of course, kind Mr. Policeman!" she shouted, clasping her hands at her heart. "We are the most law-abiding of citizens and will absolutely attend to your order! Directly." She inched sideways. "Right now, that is. Straight home. Goodbye!" And then, for Pete's sake, she waved. "Have a most wonderful evening!"

"What are you doing?" Lewis hissed when the officer moved on after fixing them with an extra-hard stare.

"Throwing him off our trail."

"What *trail?*"

Pearl looked at him as if that were completely obvious to everyone except Lewis.

What was obvious to Lewis was that Pearl had never encountered a real policeman before. He took hold of her elbow and hauled her behind the lamppost, plopping down at its base and pulling her with him so she wouldn't make another scene—for the next few minutes, at least. His mind felt all tumbled and he needed a moment to think. He crouched there—hooking Pearl's arm with his to hold her in place—with his hands over his ears and his eyes squeezed shut.

What was going on? Only yesterday he'd been plotting a Flash at Knoertzer's Grocery, waiting for his dad. Of course, that wasn't exactly normal, not the normal of three months earlier, when his dad was home and he was going to school and doing all the usual things an eleven-year-old might do. But Lewis was getting used to his streeter life; he was adjusting. And now? Kidnapping. Scrugg. Recipe. Explosion.

Nothing to see, the copper had said. Just a gas stove. Lewis hoped that was true, that if he peeked inside the watch repair shop he'd see a gas stove blown into little pieces.

"There's the signal," Pearl said suddenly.

Lewis jerked. "Huh?"

"The whistle." She pried her arm out from his. "You heard it, didn't you? It's our signal."

"Not ours." Lewis shook his head. There had been a whistle—two short peeps, one low, one high. It was Duck's whistle, the one he used for alerting Mac to get ready for whatever it was they planned to do. Lewis had heard their routine before, but surely Pearl hadn't.

"Of course it is," Pearl answered blithely. "See?" She pointed to where Mac had reappeared, zigzagging through the departing crowd. "In 'Fateful Felony' Lola and Nigel use whistles to direct each other across the frozen tundra." She turned to Lewis, her eyes aglow. "Your friend said we were going to break into the shop!"

"He said *he*, not *we*!"

"Well, we *are* going to break in, aren't we?" she asked. "Otherwise, why are we crouched here, waiting?"

We again! Honestly, this girl was so confounding! Lewis whispered sternly, "I'm just trying to keep out of sight and you're as—as shiny as it gets! And…and whatever I'm going to do has nothing to do with you. So please, just please do what you told the officer you were going to do: go home!"

Another whistle sounded, a soft *hoo-hoo* this time, like an owl. Pearl studied Lewis intently. "Break-ins are quite illegal, Sir Nigel," she said solemnly. "You will benefit from my expertise."

Lewis scowled. He didn't need Pearl and he certainly didn't want to need her. But then again, he'd never broken into anything before or done anything illegal without the cover of the Flash. Even if he had some of his Recipe, he could hardly mix it under Pearl's pointed attention, not to mention so close to all the coppers and crowd stragglers and that annoyingly curious reporter.

And yet he had to get inside, if only to show himself that the Flash had nothing to do with the explosion. It was the only decision in this crazy day that made sense.

And so, though Lewis hated to, and feeling like he'd already crowded himself with enough partners for one day, he figured he ought to team up with Mac and Duck.

Just this once.

7

SCENE OF THE CRIME

With Pearl as his shadow, Lewis wove through the remaining bystanders to where Mac was hiding on the shaded side of a fire truck. Across the street, the firefighters were still wandering around with dry hoses and useless ladders.

Mac beamed when he spotted them. "You comin' with us, Brain?" Lewis nodded and Mac's gaze darted to Pearl. "And, uh…?" It seemed he didn't know whether to call her Pearl or Detective Clavell, so he just turned a shade of magenta.

A second, owl-sounding whistle hooted from the far end of the alley next to the watch repair shop.

"That's Duck!" Mac perked up, socking Lewis in the arm. "Means there's gotta be swell loot inside. Let's go!" Mac tucked his hands in his pockets and ambled off nonchalantly. A moment later he dashed across the street and disappeared behind one of the filling posts at the station next to the watch repair shop.

"Our turn!" Pearl went up on her toes, like she was gearing up for one of her terrible leaps. "Onward, Sir Nigel!" she cried.

Lewis grabbed a handful of pink sweater. "Wait! You can't draw attention to Mac!"

"Of course not." Pearl nodded in agreement. "We're undercover." And she repeated "Onward!" in a whisper this time—except the whisper was so exaggerated she might as well have stuck to yelling—and started after Mac.

Lewis yanked Pearl back by her tutu, exasperated. "Listen, this isn't some game! If you get caught, sure, you might get

sent to bed without supper, but Duck and Mac and me—
we'll get packed off to who knows where!"

Orphanage or jail, maybe, Lewis was thinking, but then
Pearl's eyes flashed so angrily that Lewis jumped, startled.
But then just as quickly Pearl sniffed and patted his hand.
"Never fear, Nigel. When doing things illegal, I am an expert
at being invisible."

And she fluffed her skirts and tiptoed across the street,
looking exactly like she was sneaking off to do something illegal. Worse, one of the police vehicle's headlights caught the
sequins dotting her tutu, outlining her with incandescent spar-
kles. Lewis's stomach sank, but—miraculously—everybody's
back was turned, so Pearl reached the filling posts without
anyone noticing. A moment later she and Mac ran down the
narrow alley past the watch repair shop to join Duck who
waited there, nearly indistinguishable from the shadows.

Lewis sat back, wrestling down a confused mixture of
annoyance and relief, then peeked out again from around
the truck. All the firemen were chatting with two policemen
while coiling their unused hoses. It was his turn to cross the
street. He stepped forward, then immediately shrank back.
The barrel-chested copper from before was coming toward
the truck, looking very fed up. The reporter trailed him.
Lewis held still, listening.

"I can't confirm any of that, mister, I told you," the copper growled.

"Name's Boone. Osgood Boone," said the reporter. "But
if the Flash Gang is responsible for this, they sure have
upped the ante. It doesn't make sense."

Lewis bit his lip. So the copper didn't believe it was a gas
stove? Maybe people *were* blaming the Flash Gang.

"Why a watch repair shop instead of a grocery?" continued the reporter. "Whose shop is that? Ever seen a Flash
turn orange before?"

"You're askin' faster than I can think," the copper barked,

and then drew his billy club from his belt and tapped it threateningly against his palm. Lewis winced—the tap was how coppers warned streeters and hobos to get lost. He expected the reporter to beat a hasty retreat, but the man stayed relaxed as he threw out more questions.

"Any signs of the Gang? How about Fat Joe? Rumor is the mob's got something to do with the Flash. Groceries and watch repairs are awfully small targets for them, don't you think? Or does the mob pay you not to think?"

Still tapping the club, the copper swelled his chest and narrowed his eyes. "Guess you'll have to come to the station, Mister Boone, if you want more details." He indicated his vehicle with a jerk of his chin.

The reporter smiled slowly. He had nice, even teeth. "Ah. Has the police department already decided what the details are?" He tipped his hat as he turned away. "Thanks for your time, officer. Guess I'll see you there."

The reporter strolled casually to his Buick, which was parked near the fire truck. Lewis made himself as small as possible, but as Boone passed, the reporter paused and looked down, directly at Lewis. They stared at each other for a long moment, Lewis fizzing inside, feeling like the reporter would somehow suspect him, maybe finger him as the Flash Gang right there. The reporter's mouth opened and Lewis shook his head—one sharp, desperate shake, a plea for Boone to keep silent.

For what seemed another achingly long moment, Osgood Boone held Lewis's gaze. But then, suddenly, he straightened and fixed his eyes somewhere above the fire truck. Reaching for his trilby, the reporter touched its brim ever so lightly, and moved on, humming a little tune. A moment later he climbed into the Buick, edged it away from the truck, and drove off. Lewis's shoulders caved in relief.

The firemen had finished coiling the hoses. Two policemen climbed into one of the vehicles and were leaving. The barrel-chested copper who'd been fending off the reporter got into the remaining police car that was parked down the block and started the engine. The street was almost empty.

Lewis scooted from the fire truck to the corner, dashed as fast as he could across the street to the filling station, and hid behind one of the pumps. The firemen clambered onto their truck while Lewis watched, panting. With a great, official-sounding roar, the truck lumbered away, and a dark gloom descended on the lot, the buildings, and the surrounding street.

Lewis started for the alley, but another of Duck's whistles pierced the air, stopping him in his tracks. A warning. Lewis scuttled back to the pump and crouched down.

Headlights appeared, skimming across the filling station. An imposing new vehicle glided up the street—gray and wagon-shaped, with hatch doors that opened from the back. It pulled past the alley and cut its headlights. There was a silence, broken only by the purring of a powerful engine. Then the vehicle shifted with a creak and began reversing in the dark, sliding backward into the alleyway.

Lewis worked his way to the front of the watch repair shop, creeping behind a row of broken crates so the policeman wouldn't see him. He peeked around the shop's corner at the alley and the reversing vehicle, his heart thudding against his ribcage. He really hoped, wherever they were, that Mac and Duck were holding Pearl in place.

The gray wagon braked. The rumbling of its engine cut off and inside a match flared to life. Lewis could see two occupants in the front seat, one of them lighting a cigarette. Then suddenly the barrel-chested copper came jogging over to the wagon and rapped twice on the passenger window. The window rolled down. Smoke drifted out to join the smog.

The copper's voice echoed. "You're clear," Lewis heard him say. "You have fifteen minutes. Then I have to notice you."

In response, a hand extended from the passenger window

and pressed what looked like two bills into the copper's open palm. The copper turned with a satisfied-looking nod and marched back to his vehicle. He got in and shut the door with a slam.

The slam seemed to be a signal, for immediately two large, muscular men dressed in dark shirts and trousers got out of the wagon. They opened the hatch and retrieved a long, rolled-up something, then headed to the shop's rear door. They used a key; Lewis could hear them fumbling in the dark for the lock.

Once the men were inside, Mac, Duck, and Pearl emerged from behind a pile of tires. Lewis scurried to join them, and together they raced toward the window near the shop door. Duck nimbly leaped for the sill and pulled himself up to peer through the cracked pane.

"What do you see?" asked Pearl breathlessly.

Duck reported in a whisper: "Small room. All scorched on one side. Those two guys. Wait." Duck bent his head as a shadow passed in front of the window.

He poked his head up again, and after a moment, murmured excitedly, "Holy smokes! There's a *body*! Gosh, it's... he's all..." Duck gulped. "They're bringing him out! Quick!" Duck hopped down, and the four of them ran for the tire pile, scooting safely behind just as the narrow door swung open. The two men appeared, carrying between them a body-shaped lump, draped in a sheet. That rolled-up something they'd brought into the shop was a stretcher.

Mac's and Duck's eyes were wide as saucers. Mouths too. Pearl looked absolutely radiant. "'Hidden Hearse'!" she whispered. "'Frantic Funeral'! 'Deadly Do-Gooder'!"

But Lewis only felt sick. It didn't matter how exciting this was for the two streeters, or how many Lola Lavender episodes Pearl could name that had bodies. He had never seen a dead person before.

And certainly not one he himself may have killed.

8

THE WORKSHOP OF THE MYSTERIOUS JEWELER

It had started to snow. Sorry-looking gray flakes gusted as the men opened the hatch, loaded the stretcher with its grim bundle, and slammed the door. The noise echoed along the alley, hollow and finite. Lewis leaned his forehead on a tire, a sour taste in the back of his throat and a thousand gruesome pictures playing in his head, each one topping the next in gory detail, and each one involving his Recipe.

A fist thunked his shoulder. Lewis jerked up. Mac socked him again and pointed. Duck had left the tire pile and was following the vehicle out of the alley.

"I'll save him!" Pearl cried, clambering over. Lewis hauled her back automatically.

"Be quiet and wait," he gulped. He barely recognized his voice.

Pearl crossed her heart, put her finger to her lips, and then hushed Mac, who wasn't talking. Lewis hardly noticed; his thoughts were in a much more horrible place.

His dad, who was absentminded about most things, had been very attentive to his recycling experiment. He'd carefully stored the refined ingredients in those brass pots with the Do Not Touch sign and had instructed Lewis to mind them. But Lewis had gone and used the ingredients for himself, and let some get stolen, and now…now somebody was dead. How could Lewis even begin to explain?

Don't let it be the Recipe, Lewis chanted silently. *Don't let it be.*

Duck was back, looking very excited. "Vehicle drove off

with no lights on at all. How 'bout that for strange!" He scratched his head, and some odds and ends he'd collected in the alley tumbled from his grip: a button, some string, a used bottle cap.

"Is the copper gone?" squeaked Mac.

"Nope," Duck answered lightly, stooping to gather his items and stuffing them into various pockets. "But it ain't a problem. We got fifteen, well, maybe ten minutes now, the copper said, before he's gotta notice anything, remember? An' they roped off the front door, so ain't no one gettin' in." He snickered. "'Cept us nobodies. C'mon, Mac."

Duck hooked a tire and dragged it toward the shop. Mac scrambled up and then helped Duck lift a second tire, then a third, until there was a sort of makeshift ladder beneath the back window. Pearl was helping, clearly having a thrilling time of breaking in.

Lewis leaped up. It was silly to stay frozen with his gut all twisted when he needed to confirm this had nothing to do with the Flash. "Me first," he called, striding to the group.

Mac threw him an odd glance, then shrugged and took lookout. Duck held the tires steady. Lewis climbed up, wobbling on the top tire while tucking his jacket over his fist to knock out the cracked windowpane. Then he shimmied over the edge headfirst, found a shelf of sorts to grab for support, and levered himself to the floor.

Lewis swiped the glass shards out of the way with his boot and took a step into the darkness, into what appeared to be an anteroom to the storefront. It felt crowded and close and the floor was wet. Everywhere was the lingering stink of rotten eggs. *Never mind the smell*, he told himself. *Look*.

"What is this place?" Mac asked, landing behind him.

"The workshop of the Mysterious Jeweler," Pearl answered from the window. "A meeting place for traitors." She called to Lewis, "Your assistance is required, Sir Nigel. My tutu is stuck."

"This isn't a *Lola Lavender* episode," Lewis grumbled, turning to unhook the netting and getting tangled with Mac, who'd jumped to assist.

"Lola Lav—? Oh! I get it!" Mac burst out, jumping back to make room for Pearl. "Sir Nigel. From the program on Wednesday afternoons! Gee, Lola Lavender's nifty!"

Pearl landed on her tiptoes and tried balancing for a moment. "The Mysterious Jeweler is not one of Lola Lavender's grand adventures," she corrected, settling on her heels. "It is the name of the man who owns this shop."

"Really? You know him?" Mac stopped wiping his nose on his sleeve to gape at Pearl.

"She doesn't," Lewis answered for her. "The shop card said watch repair."

Pearl said, "Nigel, please. I was here with Aunt Gimlick many times. Many, *many*—"

"You weren't," Lewis insisted, then told himself to stop arguing. He couldn't think straight if he got all worked up.

Duck dropped through the window and grinned his gaptoothed grin. "Let's have some fun," he announced cheerfully. He clapped his hands and began exploring the anteroom.

When the others followed Duck, Lewis turned in the opposite direction. The room was narrow. To one side stood three sagging shelves with a tumble of rags and tins and little cans of oil and lubricant and polish. In front of him was a sink. Lewis went to inspect it. A scorch ring marred the porcelain, and a darker scorch patch marked the wall behind the sink and the linoleum floor beneath it.

Lewis squatted by the mark on the floor, looking up and down: from floor to sink to wall, and then to the ceiling, where a small, jagged hole was visible. The hole opened to the sky, where the roof had exploded. Snowflakes were drifting through it like ash.

Lewis took a steadying breath. The Flash couldn't leave a mess this big, certainly not the tiny amount that Scrugg had stolen. There had to be another explanation—lots of things exploded, right? Maybe what the copper told the crowd was true, that a gas stove had popped. Maybe the gas stove had been sitting in the sink for a very good reason. Maybe the gas stove had ruined some perfectly good eggs.

"There's no real fire damage," he called to the others. "That body probably has nothing to do with—"

"The explosion!" Pearl offered exultantly. "Of course it does. It's *murder*. The light, the stink—it's obviously the Flash Gang's doing. I am an expert on the Flash Gang, you know."

"There ain't any explosion with the Flash Gang, just a *pop*," called Duck, from a corner where he was shoving a collection of screws into his pockets.

"Exactly," Lewis said emphatically.

Pearl seemed not to hear. "They are ruthless creatures." She turned to Lewis, looking triumphant. "In fact, they might be here right now!"

At that, Mac edged to Duck, who nudged him with an elbow and chuckled. "Ain't nobody here right now, remember?"

"Murderers always revisit the scene of the crime," Pearl whispered to Mac. Mac's red color drained away.

Lewis swallowed back a retort. He was not going to let Pearl's ridiculous theories undo perfectly logical observations. He returned his attention to the scorched linoleum, and Pearl immediately crouched next to him. She stared intently at the mark, then at Lewis, and then she revised her opinion completely. "They were in *and* out," she said solemnly. "The Flash Gang is quite famous for their stealth, you know. By day, they are just hooligans branded by local authorities. But by night the Flash Gang targets enemies of the state. Tonight"—Pearl's voice rose, as did Lewis's temper—"they assassinated the Mysterious Jeweler and then removed his body!"

Lewis's cheeks grew warm. "No, th—"

"Hey! You said you saw five burlies at Knoertzer's!" Mac interrupted, calling out to Duck. "Those two guys in the van just now were burlies."

"Could be," agreed Duck.

"Exactly," Pearl said in her detective voice. "The Flash Gang explodes things by day *and* night." Lewis bit his tongue.

Pearl hopped up, looking very authoritative. "What we need is some light."

"Hold on." Duck, with the ease of one always prepared for the occasion, produced a candle stub from one pocket and lit it with a match tucked behind his ear. He brought the candle over and Pearl promptly claimed it, tilting it to illuminate the scorch marks.

"The body fell here," she pronounced, tapping her slipper on the mark and then sketching a finger around the sink.

Lewis stood up slowly, feeling the fizzing in his lungs returning. He didn't want to think it. He didn't dare—even if, all put together, the scorch marks did look like the outline of a body. "So?" he ventured. "It doesn't mean—"

"What's that smear—oh, wait!" cried Pearl. She threw herself forward, Duck nimbly snatching the candle just in time. "The infamous blue smudge!"

In the center of the scorched sink was indeed a blue stain. Mac elbowed Lewis out of the way to see. "Holy smokes, that's it! Sure looks bigger than the one at Knoertzer's, though. What's that orange ring around it?"

"Has to be because of the size," Duck said cheerily. "Maybe it's the Gang's new and improved Flash."

"Oh, for Pete's sake, it's *not* the Flash Gang!" Lewis shouted. The others blinked at him. "It's not!" he said again, defensively. Except it couldn't be more obvious. It was exactly the residue from his Recipe, splattered on the white porcelain. Somebody had mixed it right over the sink. And this time it had exploded. Taking the somebody with it.

Lewis couldn't seem to find any air. The fizzing in his

lungs had turned into popping firecrackers. He fumbled his way to a rickety chair near the window—he couldn't bear sitting on the floor that had those marks—and drew his knees, which wobbled horribly, up to his chest.

The other three piled over. "Hey, Brain, you okay?"

"Stand back, everyone!" ordered Pearl. "It's clearly a heart attack. He needs room."

"Maybe *you* should give him room?" Duck suggested.

Lewis dropped his head onto his arms. *Three breaths,* he told himself. *Just three breaths.* He heard Duck blow out the candle and back away with the others (though maybe Pearl was pulled). They were going into the next room, the one with the plate-glass window facing the front, but he couldn't really make sense of anything else. Not why his heart was pumping so hard or why he should feel so terrible when it was Scrugg who'd stolen the Recipe from him and therefore this couldn't be his fault.

Except it was his fault. He was the one who'd fiddled with the remnants of his father's experiment and come up with the most perfect diversion, the bright, stinky Flash that was somehow discovered by Scrugg. But it was only meant to help feed him until his dad returned—okay, him *and* a few hungry others, and, okay, maybe he'd been a bit smug about how much he could share, but….

Lewis peeked at the smudge, which seemed so prominent now in the dark room. What if he just wiped it away? Nobody would know…A quick swipe and then he could vault out the window; this could all be over.

Except the coppers—they knew the smudge was there. They'd probably taken pictures already and everything.

"Brain, quit panting! You gotta get in here!" Mac was in the doorway, his weasel face glowing with discovery. "C'mon!"

Wiping his forehead with his jacket sleeve, Lewis forced himself off the chair and through the doorway.

And then he stopped cold, his jaw falling open.

"Ain't it swell?" Duck said excitedly. "Wish I had bigger pockets!"

Lewis didn't reply. A glow from a streetlamp spilled in through the plate-glass window, illuminating a shop unlike any he'd ever seen. It was a mess of the most fascinating objects. Clocks, mostly, shelves and shelves of clocks—big, small, old, new. Pieces of clock, too: intricate gears, ornate faces, plated trims, hands and feet, pedestals and pendants. And then there were glass cases filled with pocket watches and wristwatches and straps and vest chains, brooches and hairpins and rings. Things glittered in the faint, snowy light coming in through the window, gilt and garnets and maybe even a few chips of diamonds. Smoke had billowed through, leaving a thin layer of soot, which cast everything in a silvery-gray hue, but apparently nothing was damaged.

"She was right," Mac said proudly of Pearl. "This is a jeweler's shop."

"I'm always right," replied Pearl, which Lewis silently, and a little begrudgingly, allowed was a lucky guess.

Duck gave Lewis a friendly nod. "Go on. Take your pick."

Pinching wasn't what Lewis had in mind. Everything was a curiosity, and nothing explained why someone would explode bits of the Flash Recipe here. Still, Lewis was glad for the distraction, glad to feel his breathing return to normal, and, truth be told, glad for the company. He turned and began studying the room like the others. Every item was old, secondhand. Some things looked quite expensive. Pearl was inspecting a glass case filled with small items of jewelry. Duck was interested in the hardware, filling his already-full pockets with wing nuts, clock keys, and lengths of watch chains.

Mac, who already sported three wristwatches, had gone to peer through the cracked plate glass at the police vehicle still parked across the street. "Think he can see us?" he asked Duck.

Duck didn't even look up. "Nah. It's too dark for him to

see us in here. Besides, those burlies paid him to look the other way."

At that Mac did a little swagger walk in front of the window, then joined Pearl at the jewelry case. "How do ya know this place again?"

"Aunt Gimlick brings me. She makes me wait outside, but I've peeked." Pearl pounced on a large brooch, lifted it up to inspect it, and made a funny face. She dropped her hands and looked hard at Mac, which caused him to go red again. "I have to spy on her, you know. My aunt is a trained agent carrying out a Nefarious Deed of an unspeakable nature. She and the Mysterious Jeweler were in cahoots."

"Holy smokes," breathed Mac.

Lewis didn't protest or even acknowledge this most recent outrageous claim, for he'd arrived in front of what must have been the jeweler's worktable. And Lewis was staring incredulously—not at the worktable, which was piled with an assortment of curious odds and ends—but at the wall of shelves behind it.

There, on the floor under the bottom shelf was a pot. Not just any pot, but a distinctive brass pot. Like the pots of ingredients Lewis kept at the abandoned factory.

Lewis went around the worktable and pushed the jeweler's rolling chair out of the way. He dropped to his knees and pulled the pot close. It was medium-sized—if Lewis hugged it to his chest, his hands might just reach his elbows. He knew it by shape, and by feel. This pot was exactly the same as the pair his dad had told Lewis to mind.

He pried off its top and a potent, metallic odor stung his nose. He dipped his hand inside. Like the two pots he'd rescued, this pot, too, held something dark and earthy. But it was neither the ash nor the sludge ingredients that Lewis used for his Recipe. This was a fine, granular substance, like sand. He put a bit between his fingers and rubbed. The grains stayed hard.

A shiver ran through Lewis. He remembered Scrugg telling Tildy he was carrying only a little bit of the two ingredients. *Didn't the boss say it takes all three?* he'd said.

Lewis put the lid on the pot and pushed it back under the shelf. He got up from the floor, feeling very strange. So his dad had refined *three* ingredients from his recycling experiment. But how did the bulldog and that snake, Pearl's aunt, know about it when Lewis hadn't? And why was it stored here, in the care of—as Pearl called him—the Mysterious Jeweler?

Pearl. Any second she'd flit over to ask what he was doing. Lewis quickly wiped his fingers on the seat of his knickers and turned back to the worktable. He started to fiddle with the odds and ends there, to make it look like he was exploring.

He tipped the gooseneck lamp and ruffled a day-old newspaper with that headline about Hitler and his growing army. He adjusted the stiff black telephone and nudged an array of delicate tools.

Then, for the second time, Lewis stopped dead still, staring down.

Never mind the third pot, there was something on the worktable, peeking out from under the newspaper, something that filled him with both exhilaration and dread. He slid the paper aside, exposing a little red notebook. He knew that notebook—he knew its thick spine and each stain and scratch on the leather cover, though he hadn't seen it in nearly four months. He reached out a shaking hand.

Duck whistled a warning, tiny and sharp. Everyone froze. Mac made a strangled little noise.

The silhouette of a man was framed in the plate-glass window. It was moving toward the alley.

The copper! The back entrance! "Hide!" hissed Lewis.

The streeters certainly didn't need to be told. Duck was already diving for the anteroom, Mac on his heels. The back door rattled as a key slid into the lock. Lewis spun in a circle, looking for his own hiding spot, then dropped to his knees and crawled beneath the worktable into what was the flimsiest of cubbyholes.

Pearl crammed herself in right after Lewis, her ballerina tulle spilling out of the cubbyhole, bright as neon. Lewis hauled her skirts in, his heart pounding. He could swear Pearl's heart was pounding too.

The door opened and banged shut. Footsteps sounded in the anteroom, then came closer. Lewis held his breath, leaned against one side of the cubbyhole while Pearl attempted to peek out. She quickly withdrew and scrunched herself up as small as she could.

Two legs appeared in front of the table. "What a blazin' mess," the intruder growled.

Lewis gulped. It wasn't the copper. In fact, there was no doubting that voice, or the green of those trousers. The intruder was Scrugg.

9

CRAMMED IN A CUBBYHOLE

Pearl gripped Lewis's arm. Lewis elbowed her in the ribs, a finger pressed to his mouth as he silently urged her to stay quiet. He wished desperately that he'd been quick enough to follow Mac and Duck out of the room. This was beyond terrible. Everything he'd just seen confirmed that the bit of Recipe Scrugg removed from Lewis's pockets had helped cause the explosion, and it was probably the newly discovered third ingredient that made the explosion so much more powerful. Now he and Pearl were under the worktable, right in front of the shelf that held the third pot. If Scrugg had come to retrieve it, he would almost certainly find them.

The bulldog's legs shifted, his fat feet pointing toward the shelves behind the worktable. He had to be looking at the pot. Lewis clenched tight, trying to become smaller, trying not to panic. He couldn't let the fizzy things build; he couldn't cough. Pearl clutched his arm tightly. Lewis gritted his teeth and curled harder.

But the bulldog didn't go for the pot. Instead, he grumbled, "I'm sick of bein' the one havin' to do all the lookin'."

The feet moved and suddenly Scrugg's hands slammed on the worktable, right over Lewis and Pearl's heads, making them both flinch. He began rifling among the objects on top, picking through tools and hardware and knobs. The newspaper landed on the floor next to Lewis, followed by a miniature screwdriver. There was a curse and the *whoosh* of a sleeve against wood, then half the items went spinning off the table and scattered across the floor.

Lewis swallowed hard. The bulldog hadn't come for the third pot; he'd come for something else.

Scrugg's feet were now turning in all directions, indecisively. Lewis held his breath, willing Scrugg not to look under the worktable.

The feet stomped angrily away. Lewis sneaked a quick peek. The bulldog was heading toward the anteroom—

Ow! Lewis just barely kept from yelping aloud as Pearl's other hand clamped onto his shoulder. How could she be so annoying? She was still holding the brooch she'd been examining, and it poked into his collarbone like a spike.

Except—crazy at it was—Lewis suddenly understood. He couldn't explain why he understood, he just did. This wasn't like all the other Pearl annoyances, this was a signal, a desperate: "We have to save Mac and Duck!" Lewis managed a thumbs-up, implying there was no need to worry—the streeters would be long gone by now. And in return, Pearl, crazy as it was, seemed to understand him. She relaxed her grip, much to Lewis's relief.

He had to give her credit, small though it was. It was excellent that Pearl, for the first time, had done all of her communicating in silence.

Meanwhile, Scrugg hadn't returned to the anteroom. Instead, he confronted the haphazard shelves piled with all the clock pieces.

"How am I supposed to find the damn thing? Where'd ya hide it?" Scrugg snarled.

He attacked the shelves, pulling items down and sending them crashing to the floor—pocket watches, a squat mantel clock held up by two golden cherubs, fancy colored timepieces. The bulldog didn't seem to care about any of their value. He just tossed more and more frantically, as if it all was in his way.

Bits and pieces of smashed clocks rolled under the worktable into their cubbyhole. The bulldog kicked at some of the bits, picked others up and threw them again, swearing furiously. Lewis's lungs fizzed as he watched. He remembered that anger; he could almost smell that sickly sweet cloth the bulldog had stuffed over his nose and mouth.

Scrugg stomped back toward the worktable—surely, the bulldog would get on his hands and knees now, wouldn't he? Make sure what he was looking for hadn't fallen?

Under the table was the only place left to look.

Lewis shrank until he was practically in Pearl's lap; she was clinging to both of his arms, the brooch still squished in one palm. He clenched his teeth against the needle-sharp fastener, against the fizz burning his lungs. The air was too close. Pearl was too close. Scrugg was too close. Lewis would burst out coughing any second. They'd be found.

Brrrrrinnnng.

The shrill ring of a telephone pierced the room. Both Scrugg and Pearl yelped. Lewis coughed into the noise.

The telephone jangled again. Scrugg moved. There was the clink of the receiver being lifted from its cradle. "Hello?" said Scrugg. A voice boomed from the other end to which he answered, a little breathless. "Yessir. Yessir. It's done. They fetched him."

The deep voice boomed again, sounding much angrier than Scrugg. Lewis pried Pearl's fingers off his arms, leaned forward to gulp in great gobs of air, and strained to hear.

"Sir, I can't help it if people saw—"

More yelling.

"That's the whole point, ain't it?" Scrugg listened, and then said, "That's why I'm here!" More booming. "Not jes' yet, but I'll find it. Yessir, I know: Small. Red. Uh, ya know, it coulda blown up too, maybe."

There was lots of yelling in response. Pearl made a face that asked, "What's he looking for?" Lewis shook his head.

Scrugg said, "Least we learned the professor was right."

Professor? Lewis's stomach sank straight to his feet.

"I ain't tryin' to be funny!" Scrugg answered to some more yelling. "I'll find it."

And then there was another pause and Scrugg said grimly, "Yeah, I heard. Look, he's just a kid. I got him once, I'll get him again."

This time the yelling was so loud the bulldog shifted, as though he had to hold the receiver away from his ear. "Yessir," he answered tersely. "All right. All right. I'll find it."

And he hung up the phone and stood there, his breath coming in snorts.

Below him Lewis sat, sick and shivering. There was no room for any more excuses. He was completely mixed up in whatever this mess was, and his father was mixed up in it too. And his father was *missing*—which was no longer a pushed-aside worry, but a huge and all-consuming one. What if his dad was in terrible danger? Was he in hiding? Being hunted? Lewis himself was being hunted, and if the bulldog had found Lewis once, he'd find him again. If Lewis wasn't safe, how could his dad be?

At that most awful moment, Pearl mouthed in his ear, as though she'd decided Lewis needed some courage: "Do not fear, Nigel! We *shall* persevere. Though my feet are so tingly we may have to amputate."

It was everything—everything that annoyed Lewis about Pearl, in one loud, certain-to-give-their-hiding-place-away whisper. He grimaced, waiting for Scrugg to pounce.

The bulldog's feet shifted, strode around the worktable, and faced the front of the cubbyhole. Underneath, the two held their breath. But it seemed Scrugg was disturbed enough by the phone call that he hadn't heard Pearl. He was tapping the desk and making his own noises—nasty grumbles, growls, and snorts. "Like I'm jes' some lackey to do his bidding. The boss don't yell at Tildy, an' what's she done?"

The feet turned and faced the shelves, then the bulldog was stooping, his great backside blocking the cubbyhole.

When he straightened, Lewis could see that the third pot was gone from under the shelves. Scrugg grunted a little as he hefted it. "He'll be thankin' me for thinkin' to collect this, at least. Can't say I'm a fool."

And he strode off, banging open the back door of the shop as he did, and leaving Lewis and Pearl in breathless relief. Except, apparently, only Lewis was relieved. Pearl suddenly let out what could only be deemed a war cry.

"Aaaaahhhh!" She exploded from under the worktable, knocking Lewis's head into its underside as she plowed over him. Lewis's coughs erupted in loud barks as he scrambled out after, gasping, "Stop! He'll hear you!"

"Hurry, Nigel!" Pearl flew into the anteroom. "We cannot lose our prey!"

"Huh? HE'S…*after*…US?" Lewis shouted between hacks. He stumbled out of the anteroom door and launched himself at Pearl as she was charging after Scrugg. He corralled her behind the tires.

"What are you doing? Mr. Scrugg will get away!" Pearl cried, but Lewis pushed her down by her shoulders.

"Listen!" he panted. Sure enough, the barrel-chested policeman was clomping up the alley, obviously on duty again, his flashlight waving. Lewis crouched tighter, trying to hold in his coughs as the copper disappeared into the shop. Moments later Lewis heard the copper clomp back out the way he came, and soon after there was the sound of his vehicle roaring to life and pulling away.

Pearl fell against the tires, moaning, "We've lost the trail of Mr. Scrugg!"

"Good." Lewis stood up and spit out the stringy things clogging his throat. "I've had enough of him."

"But this is our *case*, Nigel! They had Mr. Smolpenski *murdered!*"

"No one did anything of the sort! And Smol-who, for Pete's sake?"

"Oh, honestly. Mr. Smolpenski. He's the Mysterious Jeweler. Nigel, you *must* pay attention." Pearl became very prim, suddenly, lifting her chin. "Like it or not, we are fully embroiled in"—she instantly named it—"'The Mystery of the Murdered Mysterious Jeweler'!" Pearl ignored Lewis's expression and fluffed her tutu. "We absolutely must find Mr. Scrugg. Whatever he took has to be extremely important. Most likely it is our proof of this grisly assassination plot, and the Nefarious Deed behind it!"

Pearl was now looking both prim and triumphant, but Lewis didn't say anything. Instead, he turned and shambled down the alley, unable to take any more. He was exhausted, hungry, and furious both at Pearl and the fact that his feet wouldn't work faster, and half certain the bulldog would suddenly reappear, jump out of the shadows, and scoop him up as he did before.

"Where are we going?" Pearl cried.

"*We* aren't going anywhere!" Lewis shouted back.

She quickly caught up. "But our adventure isn't over!"

"THIS ISN'T AN ADVENTURE, Pearl ALICE Clavell!" Lewis yelled with his last reserves of breath. "IT'S *REAL LIFE!*" His chest hurt. But the stupid vise that was squeezing his lungs was nothing compared to what he was feeling for his dad. That worry was squashing both lungs and heart and all his ribs. He wasn't sure he could bear it.

"Aren't you even the teensiest bit curious to know what Scrugg took?"

"I know...what...he...took," Lewis managed between wheezes.

"Of course you do, you're marvelous!" Pearl followed behind silently for a moment. "What was it?"

"It doesn't matter what it was! It only matters that he didn't find the thing he was really looking for!"

"But..." Pearl gasped, looking confused. Then her huge eyes narrowed.

He should have known better than to let exasperation get the better of him. Pearl leaped sideways and tackled him, her fingers nipping something out of his jacket, quick as a seasoned streeter. She cried, "I knew it! Because *you* have it!"

And she held it up—the thing Lewis had seen on the desk, the thing he'd snatched up just before Scrugg appeared. The red thing that Scrugg was insisting he'd find.

His father's notebook.

10

THE AGREEMENT

Lewis leaped for Pearl as quickly as she'd leaped at him. "Give that back!"

Pearl turned, holding the notebook behind her back. Lewis growled furiously between wheezes, "It's mine!"

"Yours?" Pearl untwisted, her expression an infuriating combination of victory and curiosity.

"Okay. It's my dad's!" Lewis grabbed the notebook from her and made for the end of the alley. He had to stop there to breathe, so he clutched the notebook close in case she came for it again. It was beyond precious, this notebook that his father wrote his experiments in.

"Your father's?" Behind him Pearl had paused, too. Then she ran to catch up, her shock now changing to delight. "Nigel!" she cried. "You realize this means that your abduction, and your father, and my aunt, and the murdered Mysterious Jeweler are all connected!"

"No kidding," Lewis muttered and moved on. A drizzle of snow was still falling, more ash than white, and he was leaving boot prints behind. They both were. He thought of Scrugg again and moved to walk in the street.

Pearl was right on his heels. "Your father must be a spy. Or a secret agent. Or—"

"Those are the same thing," Lewis snapped. "And he's a professor! In the real world, jobs aren't like that!"

Pearl cocked her head and said matter-of-factly, "Why not? My father is a member of the royal family."

"Oh, sure," Lewis snorted, stopping. "And that's why you

live with that kidnapper, traitor, and…what else? Oh yeah,
fascist aunt!"

Pearl's eyes glinted. "That is only because my papa is away."

"Right." Lewis folded his arms. "So, where is this royal
papa, may I ask?"

"I told you, he's on expedition, gathering gems in the Orient," Pearl said hotly.

"The Orient!" Lewis pointed the notebook at her, accusing. "Hah! Last time you said he was on the Nile! You're
making it up!"

Pearl's face went as pink as her sweater. Lewis dropped his
arm. He might—might—have felt the tiniest bit of guilt, except that Pearl suddenly lunged and snatched the notebook
back, skipping away.

"Hey!"

"My father isn't part of the Nefarious Deed. But yours…"
She stopped in the glow of a streetlight and flipped open
the notebook to see, chattering all the while. "My, what tiny
handwriting! Is your father very small? Lola Lavender did
battle in 'Murderous Midget.'" Pearl thumbed through the
pages greedily, until she reached the very last entry. Her brow
furrowed. Then she read aloud, and Lewis stopped to listen.
"'Two thimbles of ash plus a finger of sludge produce a
consistency likened to fudge. Unstable. Most unpredictable.
The contortion of this proportion…'" She looked up at him,
stricken. "But—but this is just dreadful poetry! Sludge and
fudge? Contortion and proportion? Honestly. How does this
explain anything?"

Lewis stalked forward and swiped for the notebook. Pearl
danced away once more. "Pearl!" he shouted. It was beyond
irritating that she of all people would call someone else's
words dreadful. "Give it back!"

But Pearl's face lit up again. She hugged the notebook
into her chest and pirouetted. "Wait a moment! I understand!
The nonsense…he's written in code! Your father *is* a secret

agent! He's hidden his messages in useless verse so people grow too bored to crack it!"

"It's not code! He just puts things differently!" Lewis panted. But it was code, sort of. His dad always spoke of his experiments in odd, flowery ways. Once, he wrote the details of an experiment, involving Lewis's first effort at scrambling eggs, in iambic pentameter.

Remembering this, a pang of homesickness shot through Lewis so sudden and hard that he added in helpless fury, "And my father hasn't anything to do with your nasty snake of an aunt!"

"Let's go ask him then," Pearl replied tartly. "Let's see what he says."

At that Lewis folded over in spasms of mucus and phlegm. "Oh my!" Pearl gasped. She jumped over and began karate chopping his back, which only made the coughing worse. Finally, after several moments of gasps and retches and managing to avoid Pearl's terrible ministrations, Lewis stood up and wiped his mouth with the back of his hand.

What was he doing? His father was missing, Scrugg was on the loose, and they were standing in the halo of a streetlight with Pearl waving the red notebook practically like a signal. He had to get back to the factory—he had to hide the notebook, warm his bone-cold fingers, and then figure out how to figure everything out. But if he grabbed the notebook and ran for it, Pearl would only catch up.

So Lewis straightened his glasses and looked at Pearl sternly. "Someone died tonight. This is very serious."

Pearl was solemn. "Oh yes. Obviously. And *obviously* I've been thinking quite a bit about it."

Lewis rolled his eyes. "Don't. Don't think. Not even a little bit. What I'm saying is that it's not safe to be out here."

"It's no coincidence, you know," she said, ignoring him. "This is what happens when you deal with my aunt. You explode over the sink."

"For Pete's sake!"

"Perhaps there is another explanation."

He groaned. "Please don't tell me."

Pearl drew a deep, bracing breath, then delivered what she considered grave news. "My aunt is an active member of the Flash Gang."

It took all of Lewis's self-control not to throttle her. "No," he muttered through clenched teeth. "No, she's not."

"Then she hired them," said Pearl perfunctorily. "That's it. *That's* the explanation."

"It's not an explanation!" Lewis shot back, exasperated. "But you know what? Why don't you go home and ask her? You're the one raving about Nefarious Deeds and evil spies. Give me my notebook, and then go home and ask her what she's up to. It'll be fine. I'm sure your aunt will be so very worried about you that she'll be glad to have you back. You'll get supper and everything." The idea of a hot supper just made him angrier. "Warm bed. Warm slippers. Stupid pink bows to tie in your stupid hair!"

There was a pause. A strange expression crossed Pearl's face. She said, "But aren't you worried I'll tell?"

"Tell what?" Lewis snorted. Hours ago, he'd very much worried whether Pearl might tell on him, but that was so clearly preposterous. "No, actually, I'm not. You know why? Because your aunt won't believe a word you say anyway. No-body does," Lewis hissed through his teeth. "So go home."

Pearl looked aghast. "But—"

"Don't say it!" Lewis burst out. "Don't say your home is with me. It's *not!* I don't want you. So just go home, see? Nobody gets hurt." He turned around to leave, hoping he'd never see this girl again.

"I will," Pearl said from behind. Her voice was scarily flat. "I'll get hurt."

Despite himself, Lewis looked back. Pearl was standing very still, her heart-shaped face holding none of its radiant enthusiasm. She took a deep breath, and then she turned around slowly and lifted a handful of her curls.

Lewis's mouth fell open. In the cold gleam of the street-light he could see that underneath all those perfect ringlets were bare patches. Chunks of Pearl's hair had been haphazardly hacked or shaved. Her scalp, where it showed, was red and scabbed.

"Aunt Gimlick takes a snip when she says I'm naughty. She says it's the only way I'll learn." Pearl dropped her hair and turned back to Lewis, shoulders squaring though her voice was small. "Let me come with you, please. You could explain it to your father. You could say you met a very exciting heiress today, who happens to be an excellent cook and first-rate daughter, and would he be so kind as to look after me until my own father returns?"

She handed him the notebook. Without even a bad curtsy.

Completely flabbergasted, Lewis barely felt his hand reach to take the notebook from her. And then, when the warm leather was in his grasp, some distant whisper in his head urged him to go, to run. She'd let him. She was as still as a stone. He could just go.

But he couldn't. In fact, Lewis couldn't believe what he was thinking—no, feeling, instead. He was feeling bad, sorry for what he'd just yelled, sorry that he'd yelled at all.

He was sorry for Pearl.

Pearl Alice Clavell had made up a thousand things since they'd met, but what Lewis just saw was completely honest. Of course, that didn't make the thousand made-up things any less annoying. And he wasn't a hundred percent sure he should trust her. But he truly did feel sorry for her.

He cleared his throat, not exactly sure what to say, or how to say it. "Um, Pearl, wherever you think I live, I don't."

She lifted her chin. "Poverty does not frighten me. Lola Lavender lived with a family of beavers after she and Nigel were shipwrecked in 'Nearsighted Navigation.'"

Lewis swallowed. He rubbed his eyes behind his glasses. In the history of bad ideas, this would be near the top of the list. Still, he couldn't leave Pearl to a brutal punishment by her aunt.

He nodded at Pearl and set off down the street. He expected her to leap to join him. But oddly, she did not, and so he stopped several paces away and turned back, squinting.

It might have been the way the snowflakes glistened on all that pink, but Pearl looked like she was shivering.

"C'mon then." Lewis gestured awkwardly. Pearl blinked her enormous eyes again. They glistened too. "Come on," he repeated, embarrassed. "You can stay with me." He had to take a big swallow. "For tonight."

Pearl flew to him, nearly bowling him over in a massive bear hug.

"Quit it, please," he gasped, trying to extricate himself. "Before I change my mind."

11

SECRET HIDEOUT

It wasn't long before Lewis wished he had changed his mind. Pearl was positively giddy, skipping along, dancing circles around him. He'd lent her the notebook again in hopes she wouldn't pay attention to their direction. She was reading the last entry over and over and being exceptionally dramatic, as if that would reveal clues she was convinced his father had hidden there.

"'Expect fire and brimstone in incremental increases when combined into the Glorious Concoction. Two fingers more produce sunbursts galore.'"

Pearl's voice bounced off the empty street, the words pricking at Lewis's feelings. To hear his father's flowery way of recording information was so achingly familiar that the homesickness stayed thick in his throat.

"'This Glorious Concoction, a reduction of material pulled from the inferno's maw, will pause in momentum until the precise count of…'"

Lewis listened to Pearl reading, her voice loud, soft, slow, fast. She might not understand it, but he knew what his dad meant. The Glorious Concoction was the Flash Recipe, part of it anyway. The mixture of ash and sludge that Lewis had discovered on his own did produce sunbursts. "Sunbursts" was certainly a good, flowery term for the Flash.

And the inferno? That was easy. The professor simply meant the place where he'd begun his recycling project: Brown's Dump—where all the steel plants up and down the rivers unloaded their fiery slag into one enormous pit.

Slag was a proper word for the garbage of the steel industry, which was hot, sludgy, ashy, and gritty.

Professor Carter had been looking for ways to reuse this garbage. He'd procured a small stipend for a study from the great Pickering & Lowe Steel Company—the largest of the river factories—which was wonderful since his teaching position had been terminated due to too few students. His father had gathered buckets of slag from Brown's Dump and then tried all sorts of ways to break it down into usable material, noting his findings—in the red notebook—to report to the company. That much Lewis knew.

But the more the professor narrowed in on his experiments, the more secretive he became. He began keeping the notebook in his vest pocket, and he labeled the pots of refined material under the kitchen sink Do Not Touch. Curiosity was encouraged in the Carter household, but when Lewis asked about the recycling project, his father told him to go outside, or read a book, or, worse, to leave him alone.

It was awfully quiet. Lewis glanced up. Pearl had stopped reading and was looking intently at their surroundings, so Lewis took a breath and forced himself to move forward, even though his thoughts were reorganizing themselves in a sudden and terrifying way: Had his father given the notebook and the third pot to the jeweler? Was his dad working with the jeweler, and Scrugg, and Gimlick, and whoever was on the other end of that phone call with the bulldog? That could mean his dad was close by...Had he really left Lewis to fend for himself?

Lewis shook his head hard, as if he were shuddering with cold. It couldn't be. It just couldn't. His dad was coming back—he wouldn't abandon his son. And he wouldn't share his work like this. He'd never associated with shifty people like Scrugg. The bulldog clearly had no curiosity for the things a science professor would study; they wouldn't even know how to talk to each other.

And yet there was proof of a connection. One of his father's pots and the notebook had somehow come to be in the jeweler's workshop. And Scrugg had not only recognized the pot, but knew all about the red notebook. Scrugg had even mentioned "the professor" during his phone call.

Lewis shuddered again. Maybe they'd kidnapped his father the way they had kidnapped him, so they could force him to make the Recipe. Make ash and sludge and whatever was in the third pot. But maybe his dad had refused, and they needed ready-made ingredients. That would explain why they wanted Lewis's stash. It just didn't explain what they wanted it for.

Lewis had the horrible feeling that the bulldog was the only one who could give him the answers he was seeking.

"Do you live *in* the river?" Pearl interrupted his thoughts. "Which is lovely. I told you, I am fine with beavers."

They had turned off Smallman Street and crossed the vacant lot without Lewis even realizing it. They'd be tumbling over the edge of the riverbank in a moment. Lewis halted abruptly, and Pearl halted right next to him. He took a breath, orienting himself, then pointed down.

"There."

Pearl squinted. "A secret tunnel!" She tucked the professor's notebook in the band of her tutu, pushed past Lewis, and scrambled down the bank. Lewis slid down, stepped in front Pearl, and shifted the cement out of the way. He couldn't believe he was going to reveal his hideout to someone. To Pearl. "After you...I guess."

She crawled in. Lewis followed, then replaced the block.

They walked in a crouch, Pearl ahead and Lewis behind. There wasn't any light, but Lewis knew the path well: twenty-three steps going uphill, then the left-turning bend that brought you to the tight place where the tunnel sometimes filled with water. He directed Pearl with whispers and nudges. She chattered back happily.

"Secret tunnels are very important, you know. We have one at home. One tunnel and two libraries. Papa says two libraries per household are adequate to keep one entertained during the winter, though he hardly has time to read. I like the radio ever so much better. I don't suppose you have one of those?" she asked hopefully.

"Your head." Lewis nudged her away from a large rusty bolt that stuck out of the casing.

"My Nigel," Pearl sighed, as if he'd just saved her from one of Lola Lavender's volcanoes or something.

"Yeah. Uh, keep going. Up ahead now." A moment later they stepped out of the tunnel into a square cement pit that had once contained industrial waste. It was pitch black inside.

Lewis took a moment to catch his breath, then nudged Pearl. "Reach out your hand. There's a ladder bolted just to your left."

Pearl found the ladder, climbed it nimbly, and waited for him to follow.

They were deep inside the Grub factory now. It was a ghost of a building—picked over and then abandoned, like so many other places when all the banks and financial institutions collapsed six years back and everyone lost their jobs and money. In the faint, grayish light that filtered in from the deadlights they could see what remained: empty carts, hollow containers, rods sticking into the air like baseball bats, welding shields, and pieces of rubberized aprons.

Lewis navigated Pearl through the mess toward an elevator shaft where a tumble of metal drums was just high enough to reach the main floor opening. He climbed up one side extra carefully to show her the way, then reached for her hand. Pearl ignored him and scaled the drums as if she were a mountain climber.

When both were on the main floor, Lewis motioned for her to wait while he poked his head into a few rooms. It was habit—no one was there. Even if by some stroke of luck Scrugg had followed Lewis, no grown-up, especially a Scrugg-sized grown-up, could fit through the tunnel. He would have to cut through the fence and Lewis would know.

Still, Lewis took a deep breath.

"This way." He led Pearl to a set of stairs and up to the second floor, kneed open the door, and ushered her inside. She swished in—a wisp of pink in the shadows of the immense space. She said nothing.

Lewis suddenly realized that Pearl had been quiet for a long time. Of course she would be. This wasn't what she'd expected.

His cheeks flushed a little. But then Lewis did what he always did when he arrived. He walked over to the bank of pocked windows along the north wall and fished a candle stub and some matches from a gap in the floorboards. Then he looked out the windows, across the Allegheny, where he could see the darkened upstairs rooms of his former house. All these lonely months, Lewis had assumed—or pretended—that his father had made the choice to leave, and that he'd return when he could. That one day, Lewis would see the lights come on in his old home.

What if the professor couldn't return, as Lewis now feared, even if he wanted to?

He felt a powerful ache inside. More than anything Lewis wished his father to be safe at home. He pictured introducing Professor Harold Carter to Pearl Alice Clavell. She would probably tell him that she, too, was an expert in science, and the professor would solemnly nod as though he completely believed her. Then she would make a great show of returning the notebook and his father would be so pleased to have it back.

Lewis cleared his throat, turned away from the window, and lit the candle. The flame pushed the shadows back, revealing Pearl standing stock-still in the center of the dusty space.

"It…" she began, then faltered, and Lewis waited for her to say what they both knew. That this hideout was drab and dusty, that it was nothing. But Pearl clasped her hands to her heart and said, enraptured: "Oh, Nigel, this is absolutely *enchanting!*" Exploring, she walked to the broad column on the left side of the space, which was dotted with pegs and makeshift shelves. Pearl ran a finger across Lewis's folded extra sweater and the flannel pullover he used as a nightshirt. Then she moved to the open cabinet beside it and examined the bedroll and pillow Lewis had tucked up inside. "You sleep here?" she turned to him. Lewis nodded.

"You really live here!" She didn't wait for him to answer, but did one last spin, her tutu flaring and, absurdly, casting a sparkle of light against the drab brick walls. "So, an orphan then."

"My father's coming back," Lewis insisted. It sounded awfully phony.

She nodded. "And where do your friends sleep?"

Lewis looked at her, confused. "Oh," he said, suddenly understanding. "Mac and Duck. No, they're not my friends." He cleared his throat again. "I mean, I don't know where they sleep, but it's not here."

Pearl tilted her head. "I see." She paced a circle around Lewis and arrived in front of him, planting her feet and throwing her arms wide like she was embracing the whole space. "Fear not, Sir Nigel!" she announced. "Your heart is lonely no longer, for I am here."

She didn't appear to notice his wince, though they stood face to face. Instead, she pulled the notebook from her waistband and handed it to Lewis with grave ceremony. "You must be keeper of your father's code. For when he returns from his secret-agent mission."

"You're off your rocker," Lewis grumbled, but he gladly took back the notebook. He tucked it in the inside breast pocket of his corduroy jacket.

Pearl wandered now, circling the whole room, poking her head behind a hanging quilt, peeking into empty barrels. "I'm a very good—well, mostly good—housekeeper, and I am excellent company, which you already know. What we must do now is take the Blood Oath, for we are in league against two highly resourceful enemies: Aunt Gimlick and Mr. Scrugg. They want your father's notebook and will not stop until they get it, but we shall brave them together and be victorious. You should probably share the code in your father's notebook so I can read it properly. After the oath, of course."

While she prattled, Lewis crossed to the area he thought of as a kitchen. He had three tins of tomatoes stored there, and two tins of potted ham. He opened one of each using his spoon and a piece of brick. Then he dropped a lit match into the piece of rusted barrel where he kept a scraping of coal and tinder and an oily rag. He normally saved the barrel fire for the coldest nights, which this was not, despite the snow. But Lewis figured that since he had a guest, he ought to be hospitable. He even heated the tins of food over the flames and offered her the spoon. Soon he and Pearl were eating a meal, which, after everything, Lewis had to admit, was tasty. His belly filled well enough, and he felt warm for the first time in however long.

Pearl had likewise eaten her portion, and she now stood up, hands on hips. "I've been thinking. We need to find proof that Aunt Gimlick hired the Flash Gang to murder the sinister Mysterious Jeweler—"

"The Flash Gang didn't murder anyone." Lewis sighed. They were back to this again.

"—that way we can stop Mr. Scrugg and Aunt Gimlick from their larger plan."

Lewis sat up straighter. "What larger plan?" It was worth a shot, even a long one. Maybe somehow Pearl knew what Scrugg intended. "Pearl, what larger plan?"

She twirled away, shaking her head. "Not until we swear the Blood Oath."

"The what?" Lewis threw his hands up. "Okay, fine. What are we doing?"

"It's called a Blood Oath, Nigel. We swear it to each other."

"What do we swear?"

She twirled back. "Fealty."

"What?"

"It's our friendship bond. So that we are ever loyal to each other."

"Oh, for Pete's sake," Lewis groaned. "Fine. Fine. I—"

"Oooohhh! Let me!" Pearl thunked to her knees and put one hand behind her back and one across her heart. "I, Pearl Alice Clavell, of truest heart, do hereby claim undying loyalty and allegiance—"

"Those are the same thing."

"I hereby claim loyalty and allegiance and faithfulness to Sir Nigel—what's your last name?"

Lewis snorted. "Why? You don't even get my first name right."

Pearl ignored that. "To my Sir Nigel. By this I mean, I shall never tell my aunt or Mr. Scrugg where to find his lair. Further, I shall let no person abscond with my very best friend and most trusted ally!" She stood up, her voice rising. "I will swim through a thousand piranhas. I will climb six mountaintops. I will starve one hundred days. My Sir Nigel shall *never* be taken under my watch!"

Lewis asked, "Are you done?"

"Now we have to prick our fingers."

"No. We don't."

When she protested, Lewis made a very rational explanation about rusty nails and germs. Finally Pearl relented and agreed to lock pinkies. They looked each other in the eye and recited, "Till death or expiration!" Lewis wasn't sure how expiration was different than death, but he really wanted to hear what she knew so he chanted along.

"Okay," he said when they'd finished. "What's Scrugg up to?"

Pearl stretched her legs out, rested on the backs of her forearms, and swished her feet about. "I don't know. Not exactly."

"Pearl!"

"What I do know is that Mr. Scrugg sometimes comes to the house." She glanced up from her feet. "Aunt Gimlick locks me in the closet, of course, but I listen."

"You weren't in the closet the day he brought me to your house."

"That's because Mr. Scrugg surprised her. She hadn't time. She regretted that."

Lewis had to smile, remembering the sounds of furniture crashing and Aunt Gimlick's ever-rising hysteria.

"Sometimes henchmen deliver envelopes. Aunt Gimlick takes the envelopes and locks them in the desk drawer while she gets ready. I inspect them, of course."

"How, if they're locked up?"

Pearl sighed extra-long. "Have you never heard of a bobby pin? Lola Lavender's favorite unlocking device. Anyway, the envelopes have symbols on them."

She broke off to look around the room, then leaned toward Lewis. "Bad symbols. *Treasonous* symbols. They're flags of a sort, but they're not American."

"Other flags aren't treasonous, necessarily. And you don't have to whisper. No one's here."

Pearl straightened. "Then Aunt Gimlick and I take a trip to the Mysterious Jeweler's workshop and she gives the envelopes to Mr. Smolpenski. Sometimes she pawns my jewels for pin money."

"So, you really have been to the jeweler's shop?"

"I told you," Pearl said offhandedly. "I'm supposed to

wait in the car, but I sneak out and peek through the windows. Tonight was my first time inside, though of course I have been planning a reconnaissance mission there for ever so long."

Lewis was trying to sort through Pearl's fantasies. As he understood it so far, both Scrugg and Aunt Gimlick knew the Mysterious Jeweler, Mr. Smolpenski, and had been involved with him for some time, which had something to do with treasonous (maybe) correspondence. Scrugg had caught Lewis, dumped him at Aunt Gimlick's house, and then brought the pouches of his Recipe to the jeweler's workshop. Then someone named the Deutscher—which could be Scrugg's nickname for Smolpenski—used the ingredient from the third pot to make his Recipe explosive, but something had gone wrong.

Lewis considered that for a moment, thinking about the angry voice on the other end of the telephone call with Scrugg. Yes, he decided. Smolpenski had done something wrong. The jeweler must have known the mixture would make a flash, but maybe he didn't expect a big explosion. Certainly not if he died.

Lewis shifted. So Scrugg had kidnapped him just to get the material from the two other pots. And Scrugg had insisted to the telephone caller that he would find Lewis again, so they wanted more material. Which meant they wanted to use it, but to what purpose?

Just great, Lewis thought grimly. He needed Scrugg to learn the whereabouts of his dad, and Scrugg needed Lewis's stash of ingredients. Not to mention that he'd also taken back his father's notebook—though, Lewis hoped, Scrugg hadn't figured that out yet.

Pearl suddenly interrupted, exclaiming, "I understand how you knew how to undo those knots!"

Lewis looked up. "What are you talking about?"

"When I rescued you, you knew how to undo the knots.

It all makes sense now. As the son of a prominent American spy, I imagine you are kidnapped all the time."

Lewis groaned. "My father is not a spy. And I've never been kidnapped before. The knots were simple physics."

"Aunt Gimlick despises what she calls street riffraff, you know. I thought it very suspicious that Mr. Scrugg would bring you to her house just to annoy her. So, you had to be part of the Nefarious Deed, just as I said."

"You said I would help you save the world, not that I was part of your nefarious-deed nonsense!"

"And you said you knew exactly what Mr. Scrugg wanted: your father's notebook." Pearl sniffed airily. "Of course you're involved. By relation." She beamed. "See what we've deduced by searching the watch repair shop? Now we shall prove that Scrugg and Aunt Gimlick had the jeweler murdered! That way they'll be locked up and can't continue with their devious plan."

Lewis couldn't help the irritation in his tone. "How?"

"We'll search."

"Oh, for… Where else will we search, Pearl—your aunt's house? Do you suppose your aunt's written an account? 'Here is How We Planned to Murder the Jeweler' by Aunt Gimlick and Mr. Scrugg. We're not searching."

Lewis felt bad about being sarcastic, but he was so tired, and so worried, and everything Pearl said made his head hurt.

"But…" Pearl sounded flummoxed. "But we can't do nothing! We need a plan!"

In answer, Lewis turned his back emphatically on Pearl. And then Pearl, after reminding him of their Blood Oath, emphatically turned her back on him.

They sat in silence, which, Lewis suddenly realized, was exactly what was needed. It was warm, they were full—he nearly dozed off himself. Sure enough, the silence of the factory floor was soon interrupted by a soft, droning, buzzy sound. Lewis looked behind him. Pearl had fallen asleep. He had a moment to himself. He stood, quietly went to his cabinet, and took out his blanket. He draped it over Pearl's shoulders and waited a moment to make sure she didn't wake up. Then he tiptoed across the factory floor to where a plywood board patched the brickwork. It looked like it was nailed or glued in place, but Lewis slid it carefully to the side.

Behind the plywood was a walk-in storage area, empty except for the two brass pots Lewis had rescued from his old apartment. They weighed almost more than he could carry. It hadn't been easy hauling them to this floor of the factory. Using both hands to lift their lids, Lewis peered in. Inside one was the sifted ash. The other was filled with sludge.

The Recipe. A sprinkle of ash, a smear of sludge—it seemed imprecise, but Lewis had practiced getting the feel of the exact amounts between his fingers. Even now, in the near darkness, Lewis filled two replacement pouches with the ingredients by feeling the weight of each handful. Ash in his right hand and sludge in the left, so he didn't accidentally mix them. He put the pouches in his jacket side pockets and wiped his hands on his knickers, since the Recipe stung a little. He started to replace the lids, then paused.

There was plenty of both ingredients. Enough to borrow little bits from until his dad came home. Except now… Lewis swallowed. He should drop both pots into the river. The notebook too. That would end any chance of Scrugg's getting them.

But that would also mean the end of Lewis's ability to pinch food—to stay solo, stay a streeter. It would mean not having his dad's handwriting, his words, or his voice inside those words, resonating in Lewis's head.

Lewis didn't want to think about starving or orphanages. Or only having memories to hold. He fixed the lids, then straightened his shoulders. Maybe he didn't have to get rid of the ingredients or the notebook. Maybe he could hide them. Better.

But then, Lewis heard a noise—a whisper of steps. A girl-sized ballet slipper sort of whisper.

"So, what are you doing?" Pearl asked brightly. "Is this your secret?"

12

Pots and Socks

Lewis hopped up, hands wide, spluttering, "What?" *Why wasn't she asleep?*

"You have treasure chests!" Pearl pointed at the pots.

"They're not treasure! They're..." Lewis couldn't think of fibs fast enough. "Antiques. They belonged to my father."

Pearl sounded even more delighted. "Antiques! Made of gold!"

"Brass," Lewis corrected, trying to fumble her out of the storage closet. "Just brass. They're nothing valuable."

"Valuable enough to hide. They might be clues!"

"They're not! And I'm not hiding them!" But then Lewis's brain emptied of explanations, and Pearl, taking advantage, rushed forward and lunged for the pots.

"Don't!" He tried to pull her away, but surprise had made him all clumsy and discombobulated. And then it was too late. She'd lifted one lid and was squinting inside. Her face contorted, and she looked up at Lewis who stood looking just as contorted, but for a very different reason.

"What is this?" she exclaimed, in the most disappointed of voices. "You're keeping mud?"

That helped. Lewis snapped to. "Uh...Yes! Why, yes, I am. My father liked to collect, um, mud. And, uh, the other pot has ash...from our fireplace."

She was staring at him very keenly.

"And I, uh, like to come, visit his...mud. When I, you know, miss him too much." While Pearl was mulling this over, Lewis hurriedly took the lid from her, resealed the pot, and steered her back into the cavernous main room.

"I have never heard of spies collecting mud," she said at length, suspiciously.

Lewis retorted, huffing as he slid the plywood back into place, "That's because my father is a professor, not a spy. Professors collect all sorts of strange things."

Pearl crossed her arms. "So where is he then? Why are you an orphan?"

"I told you I'm *not* an orphan," Lewis said emphatically, brushing off his hands. "My father is coming back. Any day now."

Pearl raised an eyebrow. "Really? Any day? Professors don't just disappear. But spies do."

"He's coming back," Lewis snapped. "Where's your dad? And I mean in *real* life, not some fantasyland."

"I told you, Papa is somewhere on the Nile. Or…"

She glared stubbornly at Lewis and Lewis glared stubbornly back. Pearl dropped her arms, her fists squeezing hard. "All right, I don't remember."

Their eyes stayed locked, their jaws jutting. One of the coals hissed in the barrel. Then Pearl broke and looked away. There was a longer silence. Finally, she added a bit thickly, "I haven't gotten a letter in ever so long."

"Oh," said Lewis.

Pearl walked over to the enormous windows. In their faint gray shimmer, she looked very alone and twice as small. "There are pygmies, you know. He might get eaten."

Lewis wasn't certain that pygmies lived on the Nile or if they ate anyone, but he realized now that Pearl had no more idea where her father was than he did his own. "He's probably too big for their pots," he said in consolation.

After a moment, Pearl nodded. "I guess everyone keeps pots."

"Yeah." Lewis grinned. "But my dad wasn't going to cook anyone."

Was. Lewis caught himself. *Is*, not *was*! He stuffed his hands in his pockets and joined Pearl at the windows. They stood by the panes of glass that he'd wiped clean to view his old neighborhood. It was very late now, and only one or two lights gleamed from the houses across the river.

Pearl murmured, "When he comes home, Papa is going to tell me all his stories at once. He has the best stories. Almost as good as the radio. And he brings back the most wonderful things." Lewis looked sideways. He saw Pearl's eyes go dreamy. "Carved masks, and bone necklaces, and beaded vases and headpieces made of feathers and glittery bits of gold and all sorts of beautifully colored stones."

"So, he's like an explorer?"

"Uh-huh. He makes maps. It's not like he needs to," Pearl added offhandedly. "He just likes to. We have all the money we could ever want."

That sounded awfully ridiculous in a time when *no* one had money, but Lewis had to forgive at least a few of Pearl's exaggerations.

"He gets very sudden impulses to travel, and then all the sheets go over the furniture and the house is shut and I…"

Pearl drifted off, so Lewis finished carefully. "You go to your aunt's."

She nodded. Lewis asked, "Doesn't he know about her? That she's, you know…not nice?"

Pearl looked at Lewis and then back at the window. "She's my mother's sister. Papa loved my mother to the ends of the earth."

Lewis nodded. He didn't remember his own mother and wondered how awful it would be to miss her on top of missing his father.

"Aunt Gimlick pretends to be nice in front of him, but really she's mean and spiteful and very jealous of Papa's riches. That's the only reason she minds me, you know. Because he pays her."

Pearl suddenly leaned forward and blew on one of the

dirty windowpanes and wiped it with her sweater. She looked at the panes Lewis had cleaned and at her own work. She put her nose to the window and squinted. "What's over there?"

"Oh. I…ah…I live across the river," said Lewis, uncomfortably. "Used to, I mean. I mean, I still do, but just not right now, not until my dad…" Lewis lifted his shoulders, then dropped them in a shrug. "I look sometimes."

"Lola Lavender spent six months on the Black Cliffs," Pearl said softly, "watching for a signal in 'Lurid Lighthouse.'"

For a moment Lewis felt true camaraderie with Lola Lavender. Then he shook himself. "Yeah, well. It's only been three and a half months."

"And?" Pearl looked expectantly at Lewis.

"And…" Lewis walked away from the window toward the fire bin. He took a big breath. "Okay, Pearl, you're right. I'm not really sure when my dad will get back." Lewis took another big breath. "He's gone and I don't have a clue where and he didn't say. And I'm—What are you doing?"

Pearl, who'd followed him, was rummaging underneath her sweater in the waistband of her tutu. She pulled out, of all things, an orange. "Here."

"Where did you get that?" Lewis asked, astonished. He loved oranges.

"The cornucopia place." She plopped herself down in front of the fire bin. "Someone gave it to me."

Potato chips and an orange from North Market. Lewis shook his head. But Pearl was peeling the orange and offering him half, which he gladly took and ate in one bite. It was smooshed and warm, but it was delicious.

Pearl tossed the peels on the coals. A bittersweet smell wafted up. "So," she said, through a mouthful of orange, "what happened the last time you saw your dad?"

Lewis thought back. "It was after supper. We had soup and then he said he had to go out for a meeting. But he didn't go out right then. He sort of paced around the kitchen."

"He was upset."

"Kind of." His father had seemed upset for a while. And then all through December he'd been awfully distant. Not science-y distracted but distant. It wasn't like him.

Pearl prompted, "So there he was, pacing around the kitchen, *wringing* his hands—"

"He wasn't wringing his hands."

"Go on."

Lewis said slowly, "He paced for a while, sort of absent-mindedly tapping the breast pocket of his blazer where he kept the notebook. Then he put on his winter coat. He... he usually forgets his winter coat." Lewis swallowed, before continuing. "And then he took a nickel for the trolley and said, 'Goodnight, son. Don't wait up.'" Another swallow. Lewis kept to himself his dad's order to mind the pots.

"And then what?"

"And then I waited for three days. And then the landlady kicked me out."

"Well then," Pearl said, much too bluntly. "He's obviously in dire trouble."

"No, he's not!" Lewis retorted. He couldn't bear to hear it said out loud for fear of making it true.

Pearl barely paused. "How else did Aunt Gimlick get his precious notebook, then?"

It was true, even if it was Pearl who said it. Lewis stood very still for a moment, then sat down next to her and dropped his head on his knees.

"I don't know." He might not have said it aloud. His throat was all clogged.

A moment later he felt a very pink arm drape over his shoulders. "We shall be brave together, Nigel," whispered Pearl. "We will find your father."

Silly as it was, it was the first time in months Lewis had been comforted. He lifted his chin and rested it on his knees, and thought about taking three breaths. But then he realized something. He tipped his head toward Pearl. "Wait a minute. What do you mean your aunt had his notebook?"

"I told you."

"No. You didn't."

"Please, Nigel, you must try and keep up," Pearl admonished, pulling her arm back to hug her own knees. "Someone sends messages to Aunt Gimlick, and she brings them to Mr. Smolpenski's shop. He's a go-between too, I think. I think he just takes the envelopes to someone else."

Lewis stared at her. "Pearl," he said very evenly, after a prolonged moment in which all his irritation concerning Pearl threatened to re-ignite. "Do you mean one of these envelopes had my father's red notebook? For Pete's sake! Why didn't you say something?"

"I am quite certain I did. An evil henchman brought the envelope just like the others. It was the thickest of envelopes, and so, of course, I investigated! And without a second to lose, for Aunt Gimlick brought it almost immediately to the Murdered Mysterious Jeweler." Pearl hopped from the ground and began to pace. "Now we have it, our first real clue, and we can't decipher it. The notebook just *has* to be a very important part of the Nefarious Deed!"

Lewis sighed. Obviously, the notebook was part of something—but that something was still too nebulous. And the notebook arriving by envelope left his father's whereabouts more uncertain than ever. Frowning, he closed his eyes, concentrating fiercely.

The more Lewis thought, the more a small thing Pearl mentioned became bigger. Maybe—just maybe he should stop trying to figure out why Smolpenski, Aunt Gimlick, and Scrugg had the notebook and start with how.

He opened his eyes. "Pearl, stop pacing. Describe the henchman who delivered my dad's notebook."

"Well." Pearl sat down. "He was really more of a hench-*boy*. They all are. But evil. No doubting his evilness."

"A henchboy?"

"Yes. Henchboys come to the house with envelopes and messages."

Lewis felt a new thread of energy running along his spine. He sat up straighter. "Did this boy look like Duck, or Mac? You know, ragged clothes and stuff. Like he might be a streeter…maybe?"

"Like he needed the penny tip for the job," agreed Pearl. "Though Aunt Gimlick does not tip." She jumped up. "That's it, Nigel! Mac and Duck will know the henchboy and the henchboy will know who sent the notebook and why Aunt Gimlick hired the Flash Gang to murder that man!"

Lewis narrowed his eyes. "We don't need Mac and Duck. I have a pretty good idea of where we can find out more about the henchboy's jobs."

"Of course you do, Nigel! You're brilliant, as always!" Pearl said, twirling around in delight. She stopped. "Where?"

"A shoeshine stand on Forbes. We'll go downtown to-morrow morning."

Pearl looked crestfallen. "Shoeshine? That sounds rather bland."

Lewis gave a half grin. "Hardly. That shoeshine stand is right in front of a real den of iniquity."

"A den! Like the one in 'Considerable Casualties'!" Pearl was rejuvenated. She smiled the most beautiful smile and spun two more circles. Then she knelt in front of Lewis to look him directly in the eye. "I won't lie to you, Nigel. Our mission will be dangerous. But I shall keep you safe. I am an expert in dealing with such villains."

Lewis grinned fully this time. "Oh, I know, Pearl. You're an expert, all right."

Pearl gifted him with another smile, and then got up, got his blanket, and spread it on the floor next to the coals. She sat down on one corner and patted the other. Lewis shifted to sit on the blanket, which was much better than the cold wooden planks. He was feeling funny, like there was some little shift in his bones or something. Pearl was crazy but she was also very ordinary about her generosity. Like it was no big deal to share, or protect, or rescue. Like it was second nature.

In a city filled with hardened, sad faces, and people desperate to hold on to what little they had, Pearl Alice Clavell was very much the opposite.

She was slipping off her ballet slippers, setting them aside, and sticking her feet close to the coals. There was a hole in the toe of one of her stockings. "Look at that," she said almost wonderingly. "Aunt Gimlick would be very angry." Pearl leaned forward and tugged the hole a little wider so her big toe stuck out.

Lewis pictured the snake Gimlick red-faced and shrieking, and it seemed the right thing to say, even as he reminded himself that he had secrets he couldn't share with Pearl. "Listen, um, Pearl. You can stay here for a while if you want. It's safer."

"Oh, I'd already decided to," she said quite casually, though Lewis thought he saw her posture relax just a bit. "But it's very polite of you to offer. And anyway, we'll soon be moving back to your home. After we find your professor-spy father and have Aunt Gimlick and Mr. Scrugg arrested for murder before they can commit the Nefarious Deed. Oh, and dispatch the nasty landlady. I will ask Papa to buy the house for you and your father."

That stung, but Lewis felt sorrier for Pearl with all her dreamy expectations. "Sure."

She wiggled her big toe. "Do you think your father would be able to darn my sock?"

Lewis rested on his elbows. "Yes, but he won't care if you have holes in your sock."

Pearl beamed. She also sank back on her elbows, and together they considered their toes.

"I wonder if Papa washes his socks in the Nile," Pearl mused. "Where would he hang them to dry? On fig trees?"

"My dad hangs our laundry on the furniture to dry," Lewis confided. "Once the landlady came to collect the rent and all our underwear was draped over the lamps."

Pearl snickered. "Papa decided to grow Tasmanian beets in one of the guest bathtubs and forgot, so when Lady Audrey visited there was a jungle in her bathroom."

"My dad blew up our teapot."

"Mine gave our llama a bath in the swimming pool."

They both laughed out loud. Really loud, and the echoes sounded like bells bouncing off the distant walls and ceiling. And so they tried shouting nonsense words like lollapalooza and booshwash to hear those echoes and laughed even harder. That made Lewis explode into coughs, so Pearl felt obliged to karate-chop him on the back, which was absolutely unnecessary and more than unhelpful. But when he'd spit out the stringy things and his lungs had calmed down somehow, Lewis found himself stretching out on the floor, sharing other silly memories. And still laughing. And when he took his glasses off to go to sleep the ceiling didn't seem so far away, the room not quite so enormous.

He was glad Pearl was there.

13

THE HENCHBOSS

The shoeshine stand at the corner of Smithfield and Forbes was unremarkable in appearance. Three chairs sat by the back entrance of a tobacco shop, with a stack of morning newspapers for sale nearby. Two of the chairs were occupied by gentlemen in natty suits while a pair of scruffy boys in too-big, hand-me-down trousers busily polished their cap-toed shoes.

Lewis and Pearl watched from the steps of Rexall Drugs on the opposite side of the street. They'd been there for ten minutes and were already shivering from head to toe. The morning was too warm for snow, but the sun wasn't making it through the haze and a chilly breeze swirled between the buildings. Lewis at least had on woolen knickers. All that was between frigid stone and Pearl's backside was a bunch of limp tutu netting.

It was probably why she was chattering nonstop, Lewis figured. He'd divulged only their basic strategy—that they were here to find the streeter who'd delivered his father's notebook to Aunt Gimlick—and she had plenty of questions. "How shall we ask? Sweet or intimidating? What if he rats on us? Do you always need to catch your breath? Should we pay him? I'm famished. How long do stakeouts last, exactly?"

Lewis squinted down the street at the large clock on Kaufmann's department store. "Couple more minutes."

"I have now counted three more possible henchboys wandering past the stand," she announced, shifting to sit on her hands. "They are not *my* henchboys, of course, not the ones who delivered anything to Aunt Gimlick."

"This is the right shoeshine stand," Lewis said, hoping everything he'd overheard from Mac and Duck was correct.

"Of course it is. You're brilliant," Pearl replied promptly. "Though it doesn't have a den, exactly."

"I only called it a den. It's not a cave, for Pete's sake."

"And if there is any iniquity, I am sure it will appear at any moment—"

Pearl stopped abruptly. A crust climbed the steps to the drugstore, flicking the hem of her thick coat away from Lewis's shoulder without a glance. Then she paused at Pearl, doing a double take. Lewis looked up, alarmed. He'd wrapped Pearl in his one extra sweater, but that didn't dim her shine very well. Passing crusts never paid any attention to streeters. But they would look twice at the girl with the blondest of curls, the bluest of eyes, and the most perfect china-doll features.

Pearl screwed up her eyes at the lady. "I have scabies," she announced loudly, and the crust, looking appalled, hurried into the shop. "Fealty," Pearl reminded Lewis as she disappeared. "She didn't notice you, so she doesn't get to notice me."

He snorted, relieved. In the sooty distance a church bell started chiming eleven.

"There." Lewis nodded eagerly toward the opposite corner.

The door to the tobacco shop behind the shoeshine stand had opened. A man of whale-sized girth appeared. He wore a soft gray suit, matching gray fedora, and spats. His jowls were freshly shaved, his hair was slicked with Brylcreem, his shoes gleamed, and the collar of his shirt was starched stiff as a board. The whale hefted himself off the threshold and onto the sidewalk, then paused, his nose tilted as if he were testing the air.

Pearl grabbed Lewis's arm, pulling him off his step. "Do you *know* who that *is?*"

"Obviously" Lewis grunted.

Her voice rose higher. "It's *Fat Joe,* the most notorious mobster in *all* of Pittsburgh!"

"Be cool, will you?" Lewis tried to pry himself free. "Don't act like you're actually watching him."

"His picture is taken all the time with all the city officials! Everyone knows he's a criminal but he's way too crafty and too popular to ever get arrested!" Then she gasped, shaking him. "That's it! Nigel, you're marvelous!"

"You're louder than the traffic!"

Pearl flung him loose and threw her hands up exultantly. "Aunt Gimlick hired the Flash Gang to murder Mr. Smolpenski through Fat Joe!" she cried, with not an ounce of consideration that the mobster could probably hear her all the way across the street. "Fat Joe finances the Flash Gang, you know. It's in all the papers."

"No. He. Doesn't." Lewis hissed. "And he's not why we're here."

"There are special lightning wicks—"

"There are not!"

But Pearl was already on to the next revelation, leaping to her feet so that now Lewis grabbed her just in case she tried running across the street for an autograph. "The henchboys' boss! Fat Joe! Ooh, your father's—"

"Cut it, would you? Fat Joe is not the henchboys' boss!"

Pearl was in the middle of saying "notebook," but it trailed away. She looked down. "He's not?"

"No," Lewis panted, pointing, not at Fat Joe but at the boy behind him. "He is."

A boy in a baker's cap and leather jacket had exited the tobacco shop. He looked about twelve or thirteen and extremely tough, just as Mac and Duck said. He wasn't tall, but rather compact and springy, as though he was made of gum rubber. The boy paused right next to the mobster without appearing the least bit nervous to be standing side by side with the fattest and most terrifying man in Pittsburgh.

Together they walked to the curb. Fat Joe said something to him, and the boy stuck his index finger and pinkie in his mouth and gave a short, sharp whistle. It was better than Duck's.

Better, even, was what the whistle cued. A sleek black Ford Model 40 Deluxe with spotless whitewall tires slid up to the curb. Fat Joe flicked a coin at the boy, who easily caught it in his left hand and pocketed it in one smooth motion. He opened the back door. The mobster heaved himself into the sedan, which sank a little under his weight. The boy shut the door, and the Ford slid out into traffic and purred off. Then the boy stretched, panther-like, and settled against a mailbox by the newspapers.

"Wow," Pearl breathed after a moment. "Who is he?"

"His name is Dwight," answered Lewis. Mac and Duck had told him. "If a streeter in this town delivers an envelope, you can bet Dwight sent him. Got his fingers in a lot of pies. He's infamous among streeters."

"Infamous?" Pearl's voice went all elated. "As in deadly?"

Lewis didn't answer. He didn't know anything for certain about Dwight; maybe no one did. Duck claimed the boy had ridden into town nestled inside the wheel of a locomotive, and that he'd announced his arrival by nicking a silver money clip from Fat Joe's waistcoat. Mac insisted Dwight had clung to the roof of the train, and stole from the mobster's personal, padlocked safe. Regardless, Fat Joe was so impressed that he hired the boy. While Fat Joe's mob worked the coppers and trash collectors and port inspectors, Dwight ran his own informal network of streeters, gathering and delivering information for a price. He sold newspapers, set up the shoeshine stand where he gathered even more tidbits from his courthouse clients, then sell what he'd learned. According to streeters, the henchboss had no allegiances; he'd help anyone who could afford to pay.

Across the street, the henchboss casually greeted crusts on their way to the courthouse. Lewis and Pearl watched as he directed the young shoe-shiners to whisk their brushes even more briskly, while handing off newspapers to other courthouse goers and slipping coins smoothly into his pockets. One customer stood to pay. Dwight offered to hold his newspaper while the man buttoned his coat. Dwight admired the man's shoes and tipped his cap as the customer left, then turned and re-sold the newspaper a moment later, slick as anything.

Pearl leaned in to Lewis and whispered, "This could get tricky, so stick behind me." And then she skipped down the stairs and across the street. Two cars nearly collided trying to avoid her.

Lewis huffed to catch up. Why did she keep acting so...so *Pearl?* As if this entire thing had been her idea. She'd probably crossed the street blindly on purpose. Probably a scene from "Toxic Traffic."

Great, he groaned. *Now I'm making up Lola Lavender episodes.*

Dwight was checking one of his employees' shoe brushes, his head down and his back to the street. Lewis grabbed Pearl's sweater. "Let me talk first!" he hissed under his breath.

Why? she mouthed back.

"Because! Because—"

"Hold it right there." The command was whip-sharp, stopping them both in their tracks. Lewis's jaw dropped. He was pretty sure Pearl's did too. Dwight's back was to them, but he knew they were there.

Dwight straightened but still didn't turn. "Peanut," he said casually to the smallest boy in front of him while handing back the brush, "grab the news for me, would ya?"

The boy, Peanut, had finished only one of his customer's shoes, but he set down the brush and turned tail, going right past the stack of morning papers and charging down the street with one hand holding up his trousers.

The customer huffed in displeasure, but Dwight smiled serenely. "Closing time," he said with flick of his head toward the tobacco shop. The customer reddened, but he left quick enough, one shoe still dusty.

Dwight watched him a beat, then called out to the other boy who was neatly folding his shine cloths. "Spike."

"Yeah, boss?"

Dwight tossed him a nickel. "Go get a soda pop."

"Swell!" Spike beamed, and he charged after Peanut, his own trousers sagging dangerously.

The shoeshine corner was now empty except for the three of them. Pearl stood statue-like and Lewis stared fixedly at the boy's back, heart thumping. There was a monumental pause, and then the henchboss turned and gave a small jerk of his chin—a definitive *Come here.*

It was enough for Pearl. She leaped forward, halting a few feet in front of the boy, then stepped her slippers together, clasped her hands at her heart and bowed. "The cat climbs the stairs and the mouse howls," she intoned.

Lewis surged forward. "What the heck are you doing?" he hissed, mortified.

"Password," she hissed back, still bowing. "It's from 'Devil's Descent.'"

"That's radio! You can't just make up passwords!" Ears red, Lewis looked at Dwight, who leaned against his postbox again. He really hoped there wasn't a password, for up close, the henchboss was even tougher looking, with his shorn ash-blond hair and eyebrows that looked silver in the light. He rolled a toothpick between his teeth, and stared right back at Lewis, surveying him up and down, boots to eyeglasses, pocket to pocket. It felt as if Dwight could see right through those pockets to the Recipe pouches, and it took all of Lewis's willpower not to stuff his hands into them, which would be, he decided, a dead giveaway. After another moment, Dwight shifted his gaze to Pearl and her ballet slippers.

He said, quite casually, "Well, you ain't here for a shine."

Pearl popped up like a spring released. "I am Pearl Alice Clavell, famous detective," she announced before Lewis got his mouth open. "And this is my associate, Sir—"

"I know who he is," Dwight interrupted, turning his gaze back to Lewis.

Lewis swallowed. It was as Mac and Duck always said: the boy knew everything.

"We're here to question you," Pearl continued firmly.

"I don't answer questions," Dwight countered.

"We can pay you."

"We can?" Lewis turned to Pearl, astonished.

"Yes, we can."

Dwight looked up at the sky, added smoothly, "Unless I feel like answering a question. Suddenly I do."

Pearl rummaged in the waistband of her tutu, and produced the gold and green brooch, the one she'd been admiring at Smolpenski's shop. Lewis's jaw dropped again. Dwight, on the other hand, didn't turn his gaze or even appear to notice, but his hand had flicked out, palm up.

Pearl passed the brooch to a shocked Lewis. "My associate shall deliver the goods when our business is completed."

There was a long pause. Then Dwight drew back his hand with an offhanded shrug. "Shoot."

"First." Pearl crossed her arms behind her back and began to pace in her official detective mode. "Did my aunt go through you or your employer"—she nodded toward Fat Joe's tobacco shop—"to secure the services of the Flash Gang?"

Lewis sank inside, convinced Dwight's gaze had just, if only a tiny bit, glinted in the direction of his jacket pockets.

"Who's your aunt?" Dwight asked disinterestedly.

"She calls herself Matilda Gimlick, which may or may not

be her street name," Pearl replied. "She is part of the Nefarious Deed. You must know of her. She has bright red hair."

"Can't say that I do."

Pearl's eyes narrowed. She looked at Lewis, then turned
and hooked his elbow, yanking him out of earshot to hiss,
"He won't confess, Nigel. We shall have to utilize our strong-
arm tactics. Here's—"

"What do you say we split up?" Lewis whispered quickly.
"I'll do the strong-arming and you go over there"—he nodded toward the shoeshine chairs—"and see if you can find
any, um, clues." If she could make up things, then so could
he.

Pearl was not pleased. "But I am an expert in the methods
of torture."

"Sure." Lewis nodded vigorously. "So, I'll—I'll signal you
when it's time."

"It's time."

"No, it's…Look, could we just try it my way? I mean"—he
thought quickly— "after all, your eyes are so much sharper
than mine."

Pearl pursed her lips. It didn't seem as if she actually believed any of his reasons for moving her out of the way,
but she answered primly, "Very well. You loosen him up.
I'll investigate." She turned and strode back toward Dwight,
making a grand show of announcing with many swirly hand
gestures, "And now, Mr. Henchboss, my associate shall make
his queries."

Then Pearl shuffled sideways, keeping her narrowed eyes
on Dwight. She walked one full circle around the chairs under the pretense of searching, then sat down and picked up
a discarded newspaper. She shook it noisily, spread it wide,
and pretended to read.

"Sorry about that," Lewis mumbled, not knowing how to
describe all that Pearl was.

Dwight rolled his toothpick to the other side. Lewis

thought for just a moment that he saw a glimmer of a smile. "She's all right," the henchboss said with a shrug. Then he made a motion that implied he expected his payment.

Lewis surrendered the brooch. After all, they had offered to pay and the henchboss didn't look willing to wait. He watched Dwight tip it this way and that and heft it in his hand to test the weight. It wasn't as if the smog could make the stones glitter or anything, but Dwight looked very professional doing it. Lewis wondered if he should mention the brooch was stolen.

Dwight put the brooch into his pocket, then slouched against the postbox. The toothpick migrated back to the other side of his mouth. "Question."

"Okay." Lewis cleared his throat. "I'm looking for something—someone, really. My father."

"He's missing," Pearl filled in from behind the newspaper.

Lewis shot a glare in her direction and turned to back Dwight. "A streeter brought something of his—something important—to Pearl's aunt, that Matilda Gimlick. It's a notebook with a red leather cover. Small, thick…" He mimed its shape, watching Dwight to see if there was a reaction. "Full of notes? Tiny handwriting?"

Dwight's face gave away nothing.

"I, uh, thought the streeter might be working for you, and that you could tell me whether you got the notebook from my father or…or from somebody else."

"Why?" asked Dwight.

"Because I need to find him."

"If your father's gone, he's gone. Worry about taking care of yourself."

"I'm doing fine," Lewis replied automatically.

"Are you?" Dwight's gaze slid to Lewis, appraisingly. "'Cause you're standin' out here in the open, and there's people lookin' for you. Bad people." The gaze slid away, then back. "You might want to ask 'Who?'"

"We know already," called Pearl, who by this time had draped herself across both chairs, the newspaper spread elegantly on her lap. "My aunt."

"And Scrugg," Lewis added pointedly.

"Floyd Scrugg." Dwight made a derisive noise. "That's nothin'. There are at least three burlies. Others too. All after you."

"What is a burly exactly?" asked Pearl, the newspaper sliding to the sidewalk.

"Tough guy for hire," Dwight said with a shrug.

Pearl shot up straight in the chair. "Nigel! We have a *price* on our *heads!*"

"Hold on!" shouted Lewis. All this stuff about being chased—any second Pearl would drag him away and he still had to get an answer from Dwight. "I need to know where my father is. Do you know? Do you?"

The henchboss looked straight at him. His face was tough, no doubt. But there was something else, surfacing briefly and then hidden again.

Pearl had retrieved the newspaper from where it had fallen and was eagerly folding it into quarters to stick in her waistband.

Lewis wasn't ready to give up. "His name is Harold Carter. Professor Harold Carter." He begged. "*Please.*"

Dwight glanced up and down the street, then abruptly straightened and tugged his cap down. He said low, "Your dad got himself mixed up with those people. Don't let it happen to you."

"Don't let what—" Lewis started to beg again, but then Pearl was yelling.

"Nigel! *Nigel!*"

Lewis jerked his head around. He gulped. A boy was tearing down the block toward them. It was Peanut, the one Dwight had sent for the news.

Peanut had gotten the news, all right. The reporter, Osgood Boone, was hustling after him, hand on his hat. They were heading straight for the shoeshine stand.

There could be only one reason the reporter was racing for them—Dwight knew about the Flash and had told Boone. Lewis was horrified. He knew. They all knew.

"Pearl!" he cried. "Go!"

He made to run, but Dwight grabbed his arm, tight. "Sorry, Lewis," the henchboss said, nodding at Boone. "He paid first."

14

Deal for a Meal

Pearl vaulted from the chair and grabbed on to Lewis, who was trying to yank himself free. "Let go of him, you cur!" she shouted at Dwight.

"Relax," said Dwight, easily keeping hold.

Between them, Lewis was being stretched like taffy. He was also spitting mad. "You double-crosser! Telling me to keep out of trouble and then bringing it right to me!"

"Boone ain't your trouble."

"Says y—" Lewis started, but then Pearl slammed her foot into his hip and was using his lower half for leverage to tug his arm away. "Let go!" he tried, but the words flumped out of him so it sounded more like *hey guh!* and the reporter, who'd arrived, intervened quickly.

"Let's keep our friend in one piece, shall we?" Boone suggested.

Dwight released Lewis's arm, which sling-shotted Pearl backward and sent Lewis staggering.

"Steady, there." Boone reached for Lewis's shoulder. Lewis shrugged away and stumbled again. His lungs were on fire suddenly, fizzing and squeezing.

Dwight, on the other hand, seemed to be done with the entire incident. He leaned back on his postbox and handed authority to the reporter by calling out over the commotion, "That's Lewis. The pink one's Pearl. She talks a lot."

"You'll get nothing out of me!" Pearl cried. "Do your worst! Sir Nigel, don't—"

But by then Lewis had begun coughing so violently no

one could hear anything else. Peanut, who'd been watching all of them with eyes bugged, jumped backward straight into the gutter. Pearl screamed something about Lewis dying of typhoid. Boone produced a handkerchief from his pocket with one hand and kept his other beneath Lewis's arm as if he might tip over at any second. "All right there, son?"

"We refuse to be your prisoners!" Pearl seethed from the sidewalk. "Unhand my Nigel!"

Boone ignored her. He watched while Lewis braced his hands on his knees and dragged in breaths, managing an infuriated, "I'm fine." Only then did the reporter straighten, put his hands up.

"Understood. No prisoners," he said.

He sounded very sincere. Pearl seemed to take this as a cue. She leaped to her feet, brushing grit from her backside. "Reveal your motives, sir!"

"Here to talk. Name's Osgood Boone, but call me Boone," the man said cheerfully. "*Post-Gazette* reporter." He looked over to where Lewis was wiping his mouth. "We've met before, you might remember."

Pearl stuck her chin in the air. "We neither confirm nor deny our missions."

The corners of the reporter's mouth started to twitch, but he quickly recovered. "Really?" He scratched behind his ear and collected the pencil tucked there. "Gee, I was sure hoping—"

Dwight, who'd been scanning the street, abruptly called to the reporter. "Mind taking your interview someplace else, News? Yer bad for business."

"Fair enough," Boone said and tipped his hat to Dwight. "As ever, much obliged." Then he turned to the children and reached into his pocket for his notepad. "Shall we take this meeting down the street?"

Lewis huffed, "We are…not…getting…interviewed."

"We're being chased by several burlies," Pearl added emphatically, moving to stand next to Lewis. "We're officially on the run."

"Is that right?" Boone looked sympathetic.

Pearl was unmoved. She gave a terribly noticeable wink to Lewis and started walking backward from the shoeshine stand, encouraging him to follow with more winks and accompanying head jerks, which Lewis considered ridiculous.

It didn't matter. Boone only followed Pearl, completely nonchalant. "Sounds like you're extremely busy. And hungry, I'd wager. You two look hungry."

"We'd rather starve than surrender," said Pearl promptly.

"I wasn't thinking about surrenders," Boone replied. And then—Lewis wasn't quite sure how it happened—the reporter had slung an arm behind each of them and was encouraging (or more like herding) them down the street. "Just concerned you'll be running on an empty stomach. How about some breakfast before you take off?"

Breakfast? At the very word Lewis's mouth started to water. Dazzling pictures of breakfast-y things, like buttered toast and orange juice and sausage, flooded into his head and filled him with cravings. Even oatmeal struck a pang of longing. The ham and tomatoes had been their last meal, the only meal of yesterday.

He looked at Pearl. She dropped the winking and was now exaggeratedly twitching her nose, which he took as a signal for yes. Hadn't she just offered to starve?

Lewis looked up at Boone. If the reporter noticed their instant interest at the mention of food, he wasn't letting on. He looked up the street with a sort of determinedly cheerful expression and kept the pace slow for Lewis's benefit, despite his very long legs. All of him seemed long—he was wiry and tall, with a shadow of stubble on his long, thin jaw.

And now that Lewis was paying attention to details, he could see that Boone's suit was wrinkled. It was the same one from last night, Lewis remembered. Had Boone really gone to the police station to ask more questions? He wondered what the reporter might want to know. He'd seen Lewis hiding.

Lewis braked and fixed Boone with a fierce expression. "Why did you cover for me at the watch repair?"

"Can't imagine there's any harm in squatting next to a fire engine," Boone said, nudging them forward.

"Yeah, but didn't you wonder why I was there?"

"Sure," the reporter said offhandedly. "But there's something else I'm wondering about, so let me buy you a meal, and maybe you'll answer a question in return."

Lewis wasn't ready to agree. But half a block later, Boone stopped them in front of a set of doors, and the smell of bacon issuing from within made Lewis go weak in the knees. Pearl's nose was going to snap if she wriggled it any harder.

Boone looked down at Lewis. "Well?"

Lewis narrowed his own gaze. He ought to stay vigilant regardless of bacon. "What kind of reporter interviews kids?"

"A good one," Boone said easily, then chuckled. "I like you. You're mistrustful."

"And extremely clever," Pearl chimed in.

"Here's the deal," said Boone, focusing on Lewis. "My editor wants me to find out what happened at the watch repair shop and why. You were there, which makes you eyewitnesses—"

"There was a whole crowd of eyewitnesses!" Lewis interjected.

"True, but none of them were hunched by the fire truck looking like they were aiming to do some extra exploring," Boone continued easily. "So, I'm just going to ask a question, you'll answer it, and I'll decide whether to believe you. To be honest, I'll likely ask more than one, because I'm usually full of questions. But you'll get a plate of hot food regardless, even if you lie. Not a bad deal. So? What do you say?"

Lewis kept his gaze narrowed, a little battle of conscience

raging inside of him. Hadn't Scrugg offered him a deal for his Recipe? Look where that had landed him. And what if the reporter's question was about the Flash Gang? How well could he lie about his secret identity? Honestly, he was having enough trouble fibbing to Pearl. What if the reporter asked him to empty his pockets?

On the other hand, Boone's offer seemed, in fact, a very good deal. It gave Lewis another day of food before he'd have to figure out how and when to use the Flash. And maybe the reporter would let slip some information on Dwight's contacts as well, since he'd obviously had business dealings with the henchboss before. Maybe he could figure out who'd sent Aunt Gimlick the red notebook.

But best, he'd get the meal. A hot meal.

Lewis stared a little harder at the reporter who stared back, waiting calmly for an answer. His eyes were kind.

"Okay," Lewis said firmly.

Osgood Boone ushered them inside.

15

Modus Operandi

The Brass Rail Restaurant sat directly across from the courthouse. It was large and well lit, with comforting sounds of china and cutlery clinking together. There were lots of brass accessories—railings, of course, and spittoons in particular. Pearl tried three before Boone pointed them to a booth.

They slid onto the wooden bench across from the reporter. Pearl immediately pulled her napkin onto her lap and picked up the menu card, as if she ate at restaurants all the time, but Lewis was overwhelmed. He could barely remember being in a place like this, if he didn't count the kitchen entrance of Olive's Diner where he practiced his first Flash. On his fifth birthday, his father had taken him to Klein's, where he'd unfortunately insisted on ordering escargots just like his dad, only to discover escargots was a fancy word for snails, but then the Depression hit, and his father's teaching job became intermittent and money extremely tight.

Lewis scrunched his eyes hard behind his glasses. He didn't want to—wouldn't think about that right now. The Brass Rail smelled terrific. Best, it was warm. He could feel his toes defrosting.

"Take a look."

Lewis opened his eyes. Boone handed him the menu, which felt extravagant just to hold. At the top of the card it said: "We will not raise our prices until workers receive more wages."

"Some places care," said Boone quietly, noting Lewis reading. "Go on. Order anything you want."

Anything. Sandwiches and omelets and waffles and hamburgers and ice cream and hash browns. Nothing on the menu came from a tin. And it cost money Lewis hadn't seen in a long time—five cents for a cold glass of buttermilk; five for a fat, doughy pretzel.

Boone grinned at his expression. "Go on," he urged, as a waitress in a stiff apron came over. "Anything."

Soon Lewis had a sizzling plate of eggs and bacon and hotcakes and a Nehi root beer. Boone had toast and black coffee. Pearl asked for two slices of lemon meringue pie and hot chocolate with extra whipped cream. The frothy crown of meringue looked tempting, but Lewis was thrilled with his breakfast. It was almost too good to believe that he'd get to eat it. He'd been living on smells for so long.

Still, Lewis couldn't help adding up the cost once more before he tucked in, calculating that Boone was spending over two dollars on this meal to ask one question.

It was going to be some question.

Don't tell him anything about the Flash Gang. You don't have to say anything about the truth, he reminded himself. *And start eating now, before he asks and you have to make a quick getaway.*

Lewis picked up his knife and fork.

But Boone didn't ask his question. It seemed the reporter was letting them eat. And Lewis had never tasted a more delicious meal in his life. The bacon was crisp and the eggs were fried just right, and all of it piping hot so that it steamed his glasses. Pearl didn't look up from her plate. He could hear her humming a little with each mouthful, like she was savoring the sweetness. It wouldn't surprise him if nasty Aunt Gimlick allowed no sugar in her household.

Lewis polished off the bacon and eggs and was digging into the hotcakes, feeling that wonderful filled-belly sensation, and so he dared to venture a glance across the table, curious about the reporter. For all his bravado with the copper and Scrugg, Boone seemed neither aggressive nor mean.

He had a nice face. And he had now, too, a faraway look, as though he was thinking hard about things that weren't right in front of him. His hair was very dark, a chunk of which kept falling into his eyes as he stared at his coffee. His nose was thin like the rest of him and looked as if it might have gotten broken once or twice. Maybe being a reporter was dangerous, even if it did afford restaurant meals.

Boone glanced up before Lewis could fully drop his gaze. "Ready?"

The reporter's tone was kind, and he'd smiled, which wasn't fair. Of course Lewis wasn't ready; he'd much rather finish breakfast and not answer anything at all. But he nodded his head and prepared what he hoped was a blank expression for any Flash Gang reference. Lewis looked up just as Pearl set her fork down.

"I'll have you know," she announced, "the jeweler's back window was *already* nearly broken when we climbed in."

Lewis's breath went out so hard he burst out coughing.

"Okay," Boone replied, watching Lewis carefully. When Lewis cleared his throat and nodded, Boone asked them. "So. Was there a body?"

Lewis and Pearl sat stunned. It wasn't a question either of them was prepared for.

"I'm not here to get you kids in trouble," Boone supplied, as if he thought they didn't understand him. "But since she"—he pointed at Pearl—"says you got inside the watch shop, I'm wondering: Did you see a body?"

Lewis considered his options. He could answer, but he could also lie. It depended on what the reporter was trying to do. If Osgood Boone wanted to pin a murder on the Flash Gang, then he should definitely lie. But if—

"Of course we did," answered Pearl.

"Pearl!" Lewis glared. Had she no consideration for all his careful mental calculations?

Regardless, it was clearly the answer the reporter was

hoping for. Boone set down his coffee and pulled out his notepad and pencil. "All right, then. Tell me about it."

"Oh," sighed Pearl. "It was extremely gruesome." She popped a mound of meringue into her mouth.

"You don't know that," Lewis hissed.

"Duck said."

"Shhh!"

"Who is Duck?" asked Boone.

"Nobody," said Lewis.

"Our friend," said Pearl.

Boone gave a lopsided grin. "Your friend is a nobody?"

Actually, Duck would say that was exactly what he was, and with his own returning grin, thought Lewis. But Pearl only leaned sideways and whispered as loudly as ever, "So? They might get a meal too." And she proceeded to tell Boone about the tire pile and the cracked window and the hatch-backed auto and the body and Duck's gory bits and the draped sheet, all while adding far more detail than Lewis recalled himself.

The reporter scribbled in his notepad. "So, you saw two men talking to an officer."

"They *paid* him *off*," Pearl said knowingly.

Boone nodded. "I got that part. But then the men—not the officer—the two men took the body away." He looked up for confirmation. "Do you remember what the men looked like?"

"Big," Pearl answered through a spoonful of pie, clearly enjoying herself. Then her eyes widened, and she gave a custardy gasp and turned to Lewis. "They were *burlies!*"

They were, thought Lewis, suddenly remembering Mac and Duck discussing this. Maybe they were the same ones that Dwight had said were after them.

Boone looked concerned. "That sounds scary."

"It was," Pearl confirmed with a theatrical shiver and grabbing for Lewis's arm so he had to shiver as well. "It was most terrifying. Especially when we were hiding in the cubbyhole."

Boone flipped to a clean sheet of paper and began scribbling. "You hid in a cubbyhole?" he asked. "From the burlies?"

"No," Pearl answered. "We were hiding from Mr. Scru"—

Lewis kicked her under the table. "We were exploring," he covered quickly. "You know, it was—I mean, the explosion was so...exciting. And we wanted to see what happened. And then a man came in, and we didn't want to get caught. Because...because...we were trespassing."

Boone paused his scribbling and looked at Lewis, who made his face as guilty and as sorry looking as possible. He looked at Pearl, who nodded vigorously. The reporter said, "All right then, back to the automobile. Was it an ambulance?"

"No," said Pearl. Lewis shook his head.

Boone's mouth lifted. He made another notation in his notepad. "Color of the vehicle? Headlights?"

"It wasn't using headlights," Pearl announced enthusiastically. "Just like 'Darker Danger.'"

Lewis sighed. "Okay, yeah, um...That's a radio show—"

"*The Adventures of Lola Lavender.*" Boone glanced up from his notepad. "Episode twenty-one. I liked that one."

Lewis's growing opinion of Boone took a hit, while Pearl seemed to expand with joy. Her voice went all warbly. "Oh *yes!* When the evildoers murdered the poor little hunchback and drove him to the sea in a car with no headlights, but Lola recovered his body so he could have a proper burial." She gave a dramatic sigh, then bounced on the bench. "That's it! They're going to dump Mr. Smolpenski's body into the sea! Write that down!"

"We're not anywhere close to the sea, Pearl," said Lewis.

Boone's eyebrows furrowed. "Smolpenski. The jeweler."

"Yes." Pearl tapped the notepad. "He repaired clocks and sold pawned jewelry, but I am certain he was in cahoots with my traitorous aunt. Still, it's a most dreadful end, to be blown to bits by the Flash Gang."

Now she'd done it. Lewis gave her another swift kick under the table, hissing, "For the last time, it wasn't the Flash Gang!"

Pearl pursed her lips. "We *both* saw the *in*famous blue smudge on the floor. And there was the rotten egg smell."

Boone looked extremely interested at that. Lewis said hotly, "Lots of things could make that smell!"

"Name one," said Pearl.

"Rotten eggs!"

Pearl rolled her eyes. "How about the huge umbrella of light overhead? How's that *not* the Flash Gang?"

"How *is* it? The Flash Gang flash is never that big. And besides, they only pinch food."

"Maybe they're not hungry anymore. Maybe they want gold."

"Gold!" Lewis snorted derisively.

"Or jewels," Pearl seethed back.

"When did the Flash Gang ever hurt anyone?"

That was Boone. The reporter asked it, Lewis thought, the way his dad would have, as if he himself was pondering the answer. He also said it firmly enough that Pearl shut up. Lewis's estimation of the reporter soared. He beamed victoriously at Pearl.

Boone smiled. "I've been reporting on the Flash Gang for months, and…" He leaned toward Pearl. "I'm sorry to disappoint you, but other than the unconfirmed blue smudge, nothing in last night's blast is consistent with their MO."

Pearl turned to Lewis. "That's modus operandi. It means their usual behavior," she announced for his benefit, since he obviously did not listen to Lola Lavender adventures. Lewis didn't care how superior she sounded, the relief he was feeling—that the reporter wasn't assuming the guilt of the Flash Gang—was indescribable. He went back to his hotcakes.

Pearl leaned in toward the reporter. "A most astute observation," she said gravely. "But *somebody* murdered Mr. Smolpenski."

Boone looked at Pearl for a good long moment. He looked at Lewis (who stopped chewing) for another long moment. Then he folded his hands over his notebook and said, thoughtfully, "I suppose…it would be all right to tell you something."

"What?" Pearl exploded, her arms flinging wide, knocking Lewis's fork from his grasp. "Is it about the traitors? The treasonous Nefarious Deed? The missing professor? The mob? What? Tell us! *What?*"

Lewis retrieved his fork while Boone returned to his notebook, scribbling down each of the ideas Pearl had just thrown out. "I was…er…going to say things aren't always as they appear, but now"—he scanned all he'd just written—"now, it seems, I have a lot more questions."

"What things?" begged Pearl.

Boone hesitated then said, "Episode fifty-seven."

Pearl's bow mouth went perfectly round. "'Turbulent Twins'!"

Boone nodded and Pearl looked ecstatic. Lewis groaned.

Pearl spun to face Lewis, her eyes glowing. "That means someone *else* was in the jeweler's shop when it exploded. Mr. Smolpenski is alive!"

Lewis practically spit out his hotcakes.

"Yes, indeed," said Boone. "At least as of midnight."

"How?" Pearl demanded, turning back to Boone. "Did you see him?"

"Apparently the jeweler is out of town. I overheard the police speaking with him last night by telephone, when I was, shall we say, trying to make myself useful at the police station. Mr. Smolpenski did not sound pleased to learn about the incident, but of course that's just my opinion. I'll track him down later to get his full reaction."

"So who died?" asked Pearl turning to Lewis, blinking.

But Lewis just blinked back, trying to swallow food that was now threatening to come up. The moment Pearl had pronounced Mr. Smolpenski alive, a terrible, paralyzing thought had struck him:

What if the body was his father's?

That would explain why the third pot was at the shop— maybe his father had been at the watch repair the whole time, until the moment he exploded himself with his own experiment. But then why did the notebook come from Gimlick; wouldn't his father have kept it? And more importantly, why would his dad leave him to fend for himself, just to continue working so close to home?

Why would his dad leave him for some crazy experiment and die?

"Are you all right, Lewis?" asked Boone.

But Lewis couldn't answer. He put his head down on the table, for it suddenly felt too heavy to hold up. His father dead? Dead? Lewis could hear the horrible words he was thinking, but his brain wouldn't accept the idea. Above him Boone was shifting, probably coming over to sit by him. Lewis couldn't move, couldn't pretend that he was fine.

And then suddenly there was a great commotion in the restaurant. The front doors swung open and Spike crashed inside, running to their table, panting and red-faced.

"Get up!" he said urgently. "Dwight says you gotta go right now!" He grabbed Lewis's sleeve and dragged him from the booth.

"Burlies?" gasped Pearl, and Spike shot her a look that confirmed it. She leaped to her feet, cramming the last bit of pie in her mouth, and followed Lewis off the bench. Boone was up too, no questions this time, just pulling a fistful of coins and bills from a trouser pocket and dropping three dollars on the table.

"Not the front," Spike hissed, pushing them toward the

back. "You gotta follow me." He swiped Lewis's unfinished bottle of root beer, nodded at the goggling waitress, then led them between the tables and spittoons, right through the swinging doors to the kitchen and all the way out the back and down a staircase into the alley. "Okay. Stay here," he commanded, then zoomed off toward the street, the soda pop sloshing in his hand.

There were burlies. Two of them, in rolled-up shirtsleeves despite the frosty weather, trudging right past Spike and the alley, aiming for the Brass Rail entrance. They were broad and thick-necked and altogether scary-looking. Lewis heard Pearl suck in her breath.

Boone caught them both by the shoulders, pulling them behind him. "Back up," he ordered, and edged Lewis and Pearl backward into a niche underneath the steps they'd just descended. Boone crouched to fit. It was dank and slimy.

"Don't move," Boone said under his breath. A moment later the kitchen door to the restaurant burst open. There was a shuffle of heavy feet to the right, just above their heads, and another small gasp from Pearl.

I should be terrified, Lewis thought. *My lungs should be fizzing.* But all he felt was numb.

"Nah," said a thick voice above them, and the door slammed.

Boone and Pearl looked up, as if trying to see through the stair landing overhead. Lewis, staring vacantly at the street, saw Dwight appear at the opening to the alley. A thought swam through his mind—it seemed odd that the henchboss had sent Spike to warn them, and even more odd that the henchboss himself had left his shoeshine post. Dwight stood watching the Brass Rail entrance. A moment later he lifted his chin, stuck his thumbs in his suspenders, and took a couple of bold steps forward, as though he'd just been casually sauntering up the street. Then the burlies reappeared.

The biggest one clapped a hand on Dwight's shoulder

and said something, jerking the henchboss's shoulder with each word. Dwight appeared unfazed. He scratched his head underneath his cap, and then pointed farther down the street. The burly gave another menacing tug to Dwight, who shrugged, and then the two men plowed off in the direction of the henchboss's gesture.

"Not yet," Boone murmured to Pearl who was bursting to move. "Wait for Dwight."

Dwight gave a little shake to his shoulders, then leaned against the front corner of the restaurant, twirling his toothpick for what felt like forever. Finally, he gave an abrupt nod, and Boone released his grip. Pearl raced to Dwight; Lewis followed, boots slapping hollowly on the gritty cobbles. *My dad…my dad…my dad…*said his footsteps. The daylight at the alley entrance swirled like mud-colored soup.

"You saved us, kind henchboss," Pearl said breathlessly, dropping into her very awkward curtsy.

"Yeah, okay," Dwight said, still watching the street. "They're gone. Get outta here."

"Saved us," she popped back up, "*without* declaring fealty."

Dwight turned his head. Something wistful flickered in his expression. He looked back at the street, and answered gruffly, "It don't come free."

"But we gave you all the loot we had!" said Pearl.

"He'll cover it." Dwight gestured at Boone, who fished a quarter from his trousers. Dwight tucked it away, then looked directly at Lewis. "Keep outta sight."

Lewis nodded, his head feeling like it wasn't exactly attached to his body.

Dwight watched him for a moment. "You know where to find me." He shrugged, straightening his cap.

"Tell me something before you go," Boone called as Dwight started toward the corner.

Dwight paused. "Maybe."

Boone tossed another quarter, which neatly disappeared

into Dwight's pocket. "Where exactly does one dispose of dead bodies these days?"

16

A Perfectly Boring Place to Hide

Brown's Dump. That was Dwight's answer. Bodies needing to be discreetly disposed of were taken to Brown's Dump.

For an answer, it couldn't have been more awful.

Lewis pictured his father in that sprawling wasteland, full of fire pits and sallow ash and dead soil, buried in the junk he'd once scooped up for his experiment. It was horrendous to think that his recycling project was now possibly recycling him.

Pearl had no such ghastly images. "Mr. Boone," she said, "you will no doubt welcome our assistance in your search for the Mysterious Dead Man. We are expert sleuths."

"Is that so?" Boone swiveled around from the driver's seat and considered Pearl and Lewis. They were in the back of Boone's dented Buick, which smelled of newspaper ink. The reporter insisted that they stay with him, safe from any burlies, though apparently he hadn't thought through what that meant. They were parked on a side street with the engine idling, and the windows were rolled up against the cold so their breath had fogged the glass. For Lewis, it was claustrophobic. He needed to move.

"Pearl's the sleuth," Lewis shrugged, "not me. I'd like to go."

"Tell me why those men are chasing you," said Boone.

Lewis felt Pearl turn to him, but he wasn't going to talk. He knew very well the burlies were hired by the person who'd been on the phone with Scrugg at the watch repair shop, and that they were all after his Flash Recipe. He didn't care. All he cared about was finding his father, even if that meant fishing him out of Brown's Dump.

"They intend to kill us, of course!" Pearl answered, enthusiastically, for them both. "Most likely because Nigel and I are about to expose the Nefarious Deed in spectacular fashion."

"Well now," Boone said, his gaze fixing on Lewis. "That's interesting. Very interesting, wouldn't you say?"

Lewis stared at the fogged window, silently working out how to get to Brown's Dump. The pit was twelve miles outside of town, his dad had once said—

A pang shot through his chest, stripping the breath right out of him. How was he going to do this? Lewis clenched his teeth. A fizzing stirred in his lungs and he clenched his teeth harder. *You are* not *going to cough,* he told himself. *You are going to figure this out.*

"I'd like to go," was his reply.

"Yes." Boone sounded faintly disappointed. He looked at his wristwatch. "Well. Guess I can take you home. I suppose it's safe enough."

"We have no home. We're orphans," Pearl announced promptly.

Lewis whisked around. "We're *not* orphans!"

"Fine," Pearl returned primly. "But we are homeless."

"No home?" Boone's demeanor changed. "Then where do you live?"

"The street," said Pearl.

Boone said sternly, "The street is no place to hide from those men. And it's far too cold. You must have some sort of shelter?"

Lewis glared at Pearl, just daring her to spill that as well. Pearl glared back and pressed her lips tightly together, to show that she wouldn't.

"Well now." Boone took his hat off and ran a hand through his hair. He looked worried. "Why don't I—"

"No," Lewis snarled, going for the door handle. "I'm not going to Child Services."

"Or Aunt Gimlick!" Pearl jumped in.

"No, you misunderstand—" Boone reached to stop Lewis, but then abruptly pulled back. "All right, never mind. You tell me. Where do you propose I take you?"

"Brown's Dump."

The reporter made a small noise. Lewis turned a fierce stare on Boone. "I'm going," he muttered.

"We're all going, of course!" exclaimed Pearl. "We must dig up the Mysterious Dead Man! It's likely the remains of a Nazi spy!"

"You children are not digging up any bodies," Boone said firmly, and then did a double-take and said to Pearl, pointedly, "I wouldn't worry about Nazi spies, if I were you. Not in this country."

"You'll see when we get to Brown's Dump," Pearl answered blithely.

Boone gave her an odd look, then put the Buick in gear instead of arguing. Pearl sat back and fluffed her tutu, like she was preparing herself for a journey. "I assume we have shovels?"

"We're not going to the dump," Boone insisted. "I'm for following Dwight's advice and getting you out of here." He eased the Buick out of its parking spot. "I know a perfectly boring place to hide."

The *Pittsburgh Post-Gazette* office was in a multi-story, square brick building a few blocks from the Monongahela River. Boone parked beside one of the rounded decorative archways and herded Pearl and Lewis inside.

The place was a beehive of activity, with tousled, jacketless men in suspenders and women in dark-colored skirts, whisking back and forth, laden with notepads and newsprint, urgency written on their faces. Printing presses hummed in the background, a haze of cigar smoke hung over everything, and a bitter scent of coffee dregs and newspaper ink wafted above that. Above all were voices buzzing in conversation and the *zing* and *clack* of what sounded like a hundred typewriters.

Pearl was twirling, agog. Lewis kept his gaze fixed forward. *There would definitely be a map here*, he thought. *A map to Brown's Dump.* He followed Boone up a main staircase and down a narrow corridor where the reporter opened a battered door and ushered them into a musty, dim study that was lined with bookshelves.

"I'd prefer to go directly to the dig," said Pearl, halting.

"But this will be useful too."

Lewis agreed. The library-ish room suited his intentions perfectly. He sat down on a threadbare settee and crossed his arms. Pearl crossed her arms then too, and the reporter stood in the doorway looking bemused, as though he'd corralled two odd creatures and now wondered what exactly he was supposed to do with them. He opened his mouth to say something, but was upstaged by a loud, angry bellow.

"BOONE!"

The reporter made a face. "Sturges," he whispered, just before turning around to be confronted by a very short, sweaty man whose bare head reflected light and whose plaid suspenders hung limp on his thin frame.

"DEADLINE'S IN FIVE HOURS, BOONE." The man jabbed a pencil-like finger at his wristwatch. "AND YOU'RE WHAT"—he glanced at the children—"BABYSITTING?"

"My *niece* and *nephew*," Boone announced loudly, emphasizing the relation. "They're from *Wheeling*."

"NO TIME FOR FAMILY GATHERINGS, BOONE."

"No gathering, boss. Just doing a favor for my…sick sister." Boone was now speaking very loud and extra slow. "These kids are extremely well-behaved. They're going to sit right here like I was just telling them. Isn't that right, kids?"

Sturges answered for them. "WELL, I DON'T KNOW—"

"Sure you do." Boone looked quickly over his shoulder at Lewis and Pearl, winked, and then turned and steered the man out of the room, explaining that he had plenty of time to write his usual crackerjack story, and when had he ever failed his boss?

The door shut behind them.

Lewis leaped up, attacking shelves that were full of binders and reference books and stacks of leftover newspapers and brochures and pamphlets. A map would be here somewhere—all he had to do was find Brown's Dump and then he could figure out whatever trolley or bus or incline was needed to get there. He'd use his Flash if necessary, maybe he'd set it off right there in the newsroom to pinch loose change, or maybe he'd jump over a turnstile or sprint through a terminal to avoid a conductor. Maybe he'd hitch a ride on top of a railcar like Dwight—

"Nigel," Pearl interrupted, "you're looking in the wrong place."

Lewis jumped in surprise. "Okay," he gulped. "Then where?"

"There." She pointed to a binder on the bookshelf.

For a moment, he believed her. He dragged the large binder labeled May 1934 from the shelf, plunked it on the floor, and pried it open, at which point Lewis realized it was all the *Post-Gazette* editions from that month. "Oh, for Pete's sake," he cried. "I want a map, not old newspapers!"

"We're not looking for maps. We're researching."

"Researching what?"

"The Nefarious Deed." From her catch-all tutu, Pearl pulled the newspaper she'd taken from the shoeshine stand. She spread it on the floor, opened to a back page, then looked up at Lewis, brimming with excitement. "After all these months of *knowing* yet being unable to explain! But here it is!"

Lewis rubbed his eyes behind his glasses. "What is?"

"Do try, Nigel. Aunt Gimlick is a traitor."

"A traitor," he echoed.

"Yes. And so is Mr. Scrugg," said Pearl, "though he's only in it for the paycheck. Anyway, they are in cahoots to overthrow the government of the United States. I've known it for ever so long, but now…"

Pearl's chest swelled. All her pink seemed to glow. "I have proof."

17

The Nefarious Deed

Lewis was truly confused. "Cahoots to overthrow—" he began, then shouted, incredulous, "That's your nefarious deed?"

"Yes." Pearl sat a little straighter and put her hand on her heart. "It is our responsibility to defend our most sacred democracy. And our beloved President Roosevelt!"

She removed her hand and pulled the morning's scavenged paper closer, tapping a dainty finger on an article at the bottom of the page. "Proof."

Lewis leaned over. There was a darkish photo of a man in front of a microphone, his right hand raised high. Underneath was a very small and inconsequential caption:

"Friends Of New Germany Hold Rally"

"Who are the Friends of New Germany?" asked Lewis.

"Nazis," Pearl whispered. "In America."

"America," Lewis parroted. He couldn't help it.

"Oh, honestly, Nigel! Have you not paid attention at all? *Yes*. Nazis. In America. In Pennsylvania! In Pittsburgh!" Pearl settled the May 1934 binder between them. She began flipping through the daily newspapers, talking all the while. "Last May, Aunt Gimlick took a train to New York City. She didn't bring me, which you will find surprising,"

"Not—" *Not really*, Lewis was going to say, but then he remembered Pearl and the crashing furniture and thought it was odd that her aunt had left her. "Where were you?"

"Oh, she locked me in my room for two days with a tray of food," said Pearl. "But it didn't matter. I'd already heard her planning it. The walls in her house are extraordinarily thin."

"Two days? Didn't you pick the lock?" Lewis asked, horrified.

"I did, twice, but she put a dead bolt on the outside of my bedroom door."

"Wait a minute: Last May? You've been with your aunt for almost a year?"

"Papa was home in August." Pearl brushed off his concern. "That's not the point. Aunt Gimlick attended something in New York."

"So?"

"So—*there!*" She pointed at the binder then clapped her hands in triumph. "I knew it."

Lewis looked at the page Pearl had opened. It was from the May 18th edition of the *Post-Gazette*. Another small headline, in the middle of the paper just past the New York Letter section, read:

"Mass Rally in Madison Square Garden Supports Nazi Party"

The grainy photo accompanying the article was captioned, "Friends of New Germany rally in New York City," and depicted the interior of a large event hall, with thousands of seats filling the floor and rising like bleachers from four sides of a stage. The hall was jammed with people, every seat filled. The stage had a podium and several men stood around it at attention. If he peered closely, Lewis could see ushers filling the aisles, all wearing white shirts with some kind of strap or belt looped diagonally across one shoulder. But the image that stuck out the most was the gigantic banner centered behind the stage, emblazoned with a swastika, the crossed Zs, emblem of the Nazi party. It was flanked on both sides by the American flag.

Lewis shivered suddenly, a thin, icy chill ruffling the hairs on the back of his neck.

Pearl was watching him. "You feel it too," she said solemnly.

"Feel what?"

"Oh, for goodness' sake!" Pearl stabbed the swastika. "These rallies are organized by the Friends of New Germany." She reached over and tapped the smaller photo in the morning paper. "And these are the treasonous symbols on the envelopes Aunt Gimlick takes to Mr. Smolpenski." She held her finger there while Lewis took his glasses off to see up close. There behind the man at the microphone was a flag—it had a bloated cross with a swastika in its center. "Don't you see?" she said as Lewis straightened. "Aunt Gimlick is helping Hitler!"

"You're accusing your aunt of treason," Lewis rubbed the back of his neck to erase the chill, which didn't work, "because of a flag?"

"Why else would she go to that rally in New York City? You should hear her, Nigel, ranting about how this country is filled with slobs and riffraff."

"These are bad times. Plenty of people complain," Lewis offered reasonably.

Pearl was aghast. "I'm not speaking of grievance, Nigel. Under our very noses these people are plotting to overthrow our government and make us part of Nazi Germany!"

"That's crazy. This picture was taken in broad daylight." Lewis nudged the binder. "For Pete's sake, it's in the newspaper! If this were treason, the coppers would be arresting people!"

"They haven't done the Nefarious Deed yet," she said. "When they do, it will be under our very noses, and then it will be too late for the police to stop them! And then we'll all have to wear those brown-shirt uniforms—Aunt Gimlick would adore uniforms."

"What do uniforms have to do with it?"

Pearl said softly, "You can hide the worst intentions if you make it look official."

"Look," Lewis agreed, "your aunt's bad. I know she's done terrible things to you. But you can't overthrow an entire country with funny stamps and a few burlies."

"Obviously there are more people involved," said Pearl stiffly. "Aunt Gimlick and Mr. Scrugg and whoever they report to. And then there's Mr. Smolpenski and your father—"

Lewis went hot. "My *father?*" He jumped up. "This has nothing to do with him!"

"Of course it does!" Pearl jumped up too, hands on hips. "He's working with them!"

"Don't you dare say that!" shouted Lewis. "My father was—I mean is—a professor, not some spy! He hated Hitler!" Lewis groaned at the mistake. "I mean *hates*, not hated! It's present tense, for crying out loud!"

"All right!" she relented. "Maybe he's working against them. But Aunt Gimlick gave that notebook to Mr. Smolpenski, which can mean only one thing!"

"What?" Lewis was out of breath.

"That whatever that code in the notebook explains is very important to understanding the Nefarious Deed."

Lewis sagged. Of course it was. But it still made no sense. He plunked down on the settee and tried taking his three breaths. "Pearl." He felt hollow. "My father is a professor. That code, you call it, in the notebook? It's just notes about recycling waste materials from Brown's Dump—slag, Pearl. It's just junk."

Pearl immediately sat down next to him and patted his knee. "That's okay."

"It's not okay!" said Lewis despairingly. "He's probably dead because of it!"

Pearl pulled her hand back. "Oh my," she said wonderingly. "The Mysterious Dead—oh…" And then louder, and with agonized discovery, her fingers twisting together and then clasping at her heart. "Oh—*Oh!*"

Lewis stared. Pearl in her tutu could not have looked more tragic. It was a full-on collision of the ridiculous and the horrible. For a reason he couldn't explain, he started to laugh. And then he couldn't stop. It was a huge release of awful feelings, rushing out in the most helpless and unhappy bark-like sounds and immediately churning all sorts of things in his lungs that he needed to spit out. And then Pearl was somehow pushing Boone's handkerchief at him—how she'd managed to have it in her possession he had no idea, but he was grateful. He didn't remember much after that, except that Pearl was completely silent and he was grateful for that too.

He drew the line, however, when she attempted to pull him into a comforting embrace. "Cut it out," Lewis muttered firmly, and wiped his mouth.

Pearl obeyed, but then grabbed the hand that wasn't clutching the handkerchief and held it hard. "Your father, the professor," she said, apparently reworking the story to Lewis's liking, "was bravely protecting his code from the evildoers, and they caught him at Mr. Smolpenski's and blew him up."

"Pearl."

"I'm sorry!" She looked sorry. But then it seemed she couldn't help adding, "Though it does make dreadful sense."

It did make sense. Sort of. At least it was better than imagining his dad in cahoots with Aunt Gimlick and Scrugg and the others and…Oh, for Pete's sake, he was thinking like Pearl. Lewis shut his eyes and exhaled. "I have to get to Brown's Dump and see. One way or another."

"That remains our first order of business," Pearl said gallantly. "We will dig up the Mysterious Dead—" She revised: "We shall dig by moonlight. It's best that way—the shadows will mask the worst of it." And then Pearl squeezed Lewis's already numb hand and said, tremulously, "Nigel, we shall brave this *together*."

Luckily, Pearl's next embrace attempt was interrupted by the door opening. A nice-looking lady with auburn curls and a pair of horn-rimmed glasses peeked her head in.

Pearl leaped to her feet and shouted, "We are Mr. Boone's niece and nephew! From Wheeling!"

"Really." The lady arched a brow and opened the door a little wider so that she could lean against the frame. "Quite a large family he's got, that Boone," she said, looking them up and down. "Had two 'cousins' here last week. From Altoona."

"Our sister is sick," Pearl said very gravely.

"Mother," corrected Lewis. "Our mother is sick."

"I can see," said the lady drily. "Clearly she is too sick to remind you to bathe."

Lewis looked at Pearl, and then at what he was wearing. They were far too grimy to be under any sort of motherly attention. He nodded faintly.

"I suppose she hasn't been up to feeding you either. Hang on." The lady smiled and disappeared, only to return a minute later with a half-eaten box of Lorna Doone cookies and two coffee mugs filled with water. "My private stash," she said, nodding at the cookies.

"Oh, we couldn't," gasped Pearl, batting her eyelashes all the same. "We cannot allow you to starve on our behalf."

"Aren't you a pretty thing under that layer of dust," the lady said, with a laugh. She set the cookies on the table, noticed the pulled binders, then looked at Lewis and Pearl again a bit more shrewdly.

"We're helping our uncle Boone," said Lewis quickly, before the lady could ask. "We're, um, we're—"

"Researching!" said Pearl brightly.

The lady narrowed her eyes. "What's Osgood investigating this time? Not more Flash Gang?"

"Friends of New Germany. We need to find out everything we can," said Pearl.

"Good for Os," said the lady. "Hope it's a scurrilous exposé on those fascists."

Pearl flung Lewis a very significant look and asked, "Do you know where we should start?"

The lady looked at the date on the binder. "Try October '33. Maybe December of this year. I hope Boone is paying for your help."

"Oh, he is," Pearl said, nodding vigorously. "Ten dollar—"

"—a quarter," Lewis modified, "a quarter each."

"Not too stingy," decided the lady. "Still, it doesn't get you far, does it?" Smiling, she held out a fist and opened it, revealing two dimes, offering one to Lewis and the other to Pearl. Lewis stared at the coin. Boone had given them breakfast, Dwight had warned them about the burlies, Pearl had—well, Pearl was doing her best to cheer him up, and now this strange lady had just given them money worth two trolley rides each...or some of those doughy pretzels at the Brass Rail.

Maybe it was all those gestures of support, or the worry for his father that ached in the back of his throat, but Lewis felt something inside twist open and flood his effort to speak. "Thanks," came out huskily.

"Just adding to the pot," the lady said cheerfully. "Just in case your mother stays sick a little longer."

Lewis gripped his coin tightly, suddenly knowing what he could use it for. "Can I ask you something? How do you get to Brown's Dump?"

The lady tilted her head in surprise. "Brown's— What on earth do you want to go there for?"

"Sightseeing," answered Pearl before Lewis could even get his mouth open. "We're from Wheeling."

"There would be a bus or trolley, right?" Lewis interjected, trying to sound as non-urgent as he could.

"Not directly to the dump, honey. Why don't you ask Uncle Osgood to take you? I hear it's quite the sight at night."

Pearl turned to Lewis. "I told you we had to go at night!" she said, beaming.

The cookies disappeared, and soon after Lewis and Pearl were sprawled on the floor, each holding a binder. They thumbed through newspapers, looking for any reference to Friends of New Germany.

"Anything?" Pearl asked.

"Nope," Lewis answered. "Anything?" he asked a few minutes later.

"No," sighed Pearl, then brightened. "But Kappel's is having a sale on genuine all-wave radios!"

Friends of New Germany, they slowly learned, was indeed a branch of the Nazi party. The group had been started in America by a German émigré, who was later deported for not registering as a foreign agent, which Pearl insisted was *extremely* significant. There was no mention of Pearl's aunt, or Scrugg, or, to Lewis's relief, his father. And though it appeared that Hitler's Nazi Party was a rising force in Germany, the closest thing Lewis found having to do with Nazis in the United States were a few efforts in Congress—a resolution to condemn Nazis for their persecution of German Jews, and an investigation into Nazi propaganda.

It seemed most of the country wasn't concerned about Nazi influence. At least, the *Pittsburgh Post-Gazette* wasn't concerned.

Had his father ever said anything about Nazis? He'd told Lewis the Nazi Party was anti-democracy, that Hitler made false promises and hateful accusations. He'd warned Lewis that actions spoke louder than words, and to always pay attention to what powerful people do rather than say, but his dad's real focus was on scientific advancement. Foreign conspiracy would be the very last thing he'd be involved with. Certainly, there was no mention of the waste recycling having anything to do with Nazis.

There was no mention of it having anything to do with anyone at all.

So his dad's involvement was accidental, Lewis decided.

There was a noise at the door and Boone entered, looking as if he'd been in a fistfight with a typewriter ribbon. There were ink smudges across his neck and the right side of his nose. His tie was loose and his hat had gone missing. "Story's done," he announced, pushing a chunk of hair off his forehead. "How does 'Flash Gang Upstaged by Stinkier Explosion' sound?"

"*Lola Lavender* titles are better," said Pearl.

Boone grinned. "Yeah. I'm no headline writer. Mabel says it won't pass muster. I understand you met her." He noted the empty cookie box. "She must really like you if she gave up her Lorna Doones. I can't even get one. Anyway." The reporter stood up. "Hopefully, I'll know more tomorrow as to whether what happened at Smolpenski's shop was arson or an accident, or—"

"—or part of a vast conspiracy to overthrow our government," Pearl finished for him.

Lewis winced. It sounded ridiculous.

But maybe Boone never counted out ridiculous. "Hang on. I'll get my notebook."

Lewis said, "Don't. We're not talking—not unless you take us to Brown's Dump."

"Again?" The reporter slumped against the corner of the settee and sighed. Lewis remembered Boone had been up for the better part of twenty-four hours. "Don't suppose you'll tell me why you want to go to a slag heap so badly."

Lewis and Pearl stayed silent. Boone looked from Pearl to Lewis and back again. "If I take you there," he said, "it's against my better judgment. And only to keep you off the streets. You'll remain safely in my back seat while I dig—if I dig—or there's no deal. Understand?"

Lewis nodded, too grateful to speak and knowing perfectly well he was not staying in the back seat.

Pearl clasped her hands. "Oh, good citizen, you are truly noble."

"I don't know about that," the reporter sighed. "But I hope we find what you're looking for."

Lewis just smiled back, thinking, *I really hope we don't.*

18

BROWN'S DUMP

It was dusk. Lewis and Pearl were once again in the back seat of Boone's Buick, listening to the tires hiss along the pavement. In the outskirts of the city, with no streetlamps and less soot, the sky was beautiful. The last rosy glimmer of light had slipped off to the west and night was creeping up—a rich, blue-black night.

"Look," whispered Pearl, her cheek plastered against the window. "Stars."

Lewis didn't look. The farther they drove, the more dread slogged around his insides. Pearl must have sensed this, for she reached out and grasped his jacket sleeve. He didn't push her away, though her attempt at comfort did little good. For hours, she'd managed not to mention that Lewis's father could be the Mysterious Dead Man buried at the dump, yet the very possibility was terrifying. How could he bear it if they found his father's body?

Lewis glanced at the rearview mirror and caught Boone's eye. The reporter looked away quickly. He'd been doing that a lot, looking and then pretending he hadn't. Boone had been very clear about why he'd brought them along—to keep them hidden from the burlies. But it must be bothering him, Lewis imagined, wondering what to do with two homeless children.

Boone needn't have worried. Lewis had already decided what to do. After they'd finished at Brown's Dump, he had every intention of disappearing back into the maze of Pittsburgh's streets.

After...Lewis swallowed thickly, stuffed down the dread.

The Buick pulled off the road, slowing to a stop. Lewis swallowed harder.

"There it is," said Boone.

To their right, filling the horizon, was a yawning, gray-dark pit, surrounded by train tracks. Hoppers, the railcars shaped like enormous ladles, lined up to dump slag. The slag was molten-hot, great dollops of red-orange, plopping and sliding into the hole below and sending showers of sparks into the twilit sky.

Pearl let go of Lewis's jacket, climbed over him to look.

"It's beautiful!" she cried. "Like the mouth of a volcano!" She slid back and made to open the door, but Boone caught her by the tail of her sweater.

"No, you don't!" he admonished. "We agreed. You sit right here."

Pearl slumped with a most suffering sigh, and then they all watched the hoppers head back in the direction they'd arrived. Another line of filled hoppers was arriving. They crossed paths—one glowing with fiery waste, the other darkly empty.

Boone pointed. "That's today's dumping spot. They move it each day, so all the hot slag doesn't end up in one place."

He twisted to look around the pit, seeming to tick off measurements in his head. "There," Boone said, suddenly, putting the car into reverse gear and backing up a distance. "I imagine they dumped yesterday's slag just about there."

He stopped the Buick and switched off the engine. Steam seeped from the pit here, not as fiercely as where the fresh slag was dumped, but softly—an almost sparkling mist.

Lewis's voice was stuck somewhere in his stomach. He pried it loose and said hoarsely, "Can't think a body would last long in there."

"Might find something." Boone took off his jacket and rolled his shirtsleeves, then reached toward the floor of the passenger seat. He rummaged for a moment, then came up with a somewhat battered camera whose strap he slung around his neck. He dived for the floor again, this time coming up with a handful of flashbulbs that he stuck in his shirt pocket. He bent once more and retrieved a flashlight, clicking the beam on and off to test its usefulness.

Gear assembled, Boone shifted and peered out at the pit for a lingering moment. "Stay here," he ordered, then got out of the vehicle, went around to the trunk, and removed a small shovel. The trunk thumped down, and Boone headed off, crossing a line of tracks.

Lewis rolled down the window to watch. The reporter was just a silhouette now, walking away from them, his flashlight beam making low sweeps along the edge of the dump. In the distance rail cars clanked and groaned and spilled more slag. Pearl clambered across the seat to lean over his shoulder again.

In the distance Boone paused. He aimed the flashlight straight down for a moment, then toed the edge of the pit, which caused a thick gust of steam to burst from its surface. Lewis's chest tightened. The flashlight beam moved, sweeping over the pit, then stopped. The reporter adjusted his hat, toed the slag again. He set the flashlight on the ground, pointing it at that one spot.

Lewis pushed Pearl from him and half fell over the rim of the rolled-down window, crying, "What did you find?"

"Stay there!" Boone shouted, his voice grim. He lifted his camera, fixed a bulb in its flash. There was a sharply blinding light as the reporter took a picture. Lewis blinked. Behind him, Pearl murmured, "Ow."

The word struck Lewis. *Ow*, she said—as though the flash of light hurt.

His heart began thudding in his chest. He thought of the Flash Recipe, of all the times he'd smeared his glasses with dirt for when the Flash went off. But those people—all the unwitting bystanders who'd been temporarily blinded as he raced to pinch food—they'd been affected by the Flash. The Flash had led the awful Scrugg to find him. It had drawn him and his father into something very, very dark.

Lewis's heart hammered even faster. The Flash Recipe was supposed to be so wonderful, so clever. But it had hurt others. And it had probably taken his father straight into that pit!

In a frenzy, Lewis flung open the car door and charged toward Boone. Pearl yelled, "Nigel!" but he didn't wait for her; he didn't wait for the clogging of his lungs. He ran, the ground changing beneath his feet into a wholly lifeless sort of material, as if the earth had given way to the silver-gray desolation of the moon.

Boone didn't hear him approach. The reporter was prodding at the pit's surface with the shovel and wiping sweat from his face. Lewis drew nearer, his heart bursting from effort, the heat clawing at his chest. Boone turned the shovel so that he held the blade. Carefully, he reached the long wooden shaft out into the murky wasteland.

Lewis felt like he was running in slow motion. Ahead, Boone stretched his torso over the pit's edge, grunting and slipping on the crusting slag, but then he righted himself and lifted the shovel into the air. Lewis caught a glimpse of something dangling from the handle. Then Boone examined the claimed item with the flashlight.

"Is it my dad? Is it?" Lewis screamed. The reporter looked up, shocked, just as Lewis flung himself toward the pit. He was beside himself, tears hampering his voice, his balance. "Let me see!"

"Your dad?" Boone stood so suddenly that he met Lewis mid-fling. The reporter grabbed Lewis by the shoulders and held him fast.

"Let me see!" Lewis cried again, his voice splintering into a hundred pieces. "I need to see!"

"Lewis." The reporter's grip was very strong; Lewis was

flailing, desperate to get closer, unable to get closer. Boone knelt so they were at eye level and then, simply, he put his arms around Lewis.

For about three seconds, Lewis sobbed, letting the comfort melt his resistance. But then he yanked away and made for the pit. Boone blocked him.

"There's nothing to see." The reporter's voice was stern. "The slag's too hot. Don't—" He didn't finish.

Lewis tugged, defiant, chest heaving, drilling his gaze into Boone. "Don't what?"

"Look," said Boone grimly. Then, "Here." Keeping his hand tightly on Lewis, Boone reached over and picked up the thing he'd pulled from the pit. "This was left." He uncoiled his hand and Lewis snatched it.

. A medallion, on a chain. Boone rose from the ground and took up the flashlight. Hands shaking, Lewis held the piece under the light. It was heavily tarnished, corroded, possibly by the slag. Lewis could just make out an embossed bird. He took off his eyeglasses, rubbed the medallion on the side of his knickers, and looked again.

He could see what was on the medallion now—an eagle, holding in its claw two crossed Zs.

"Lewis?"

Lewis heard his name from a distance. He'd dropped to his knees, his breath rattling in the night air. A chill ran over the back of his neck. He knew that Z symbol—a Nazi swastika, like in the photographs he and Pearl had studied that afternoon. He knew something else too. And when Boone placed a concerned hand on his shoulder, Lewis looked up at him, relief splitting his face into a smile that went ear to ear.

"This isn't his—it isn't him!"

His voice cracked when he said it. His dad had never owned, would never wear something like this. His dad wasn't here! He wasn't the body from the jeweler's shop! And that meant his dad could still be alive, that Lewis could still find him. Lewis wanted to leap and shout and cry, but since all his energy had been used up, he merely grinned enormously. Boone's face and shoulders softened. Lewis thrust the medallion at him, not wanting any part of it. The reporter took it, working the chain through his fingers as he turned his gaze to the dump. The faint orange glow highlighted what looked like a million thoughts playing out over his face.

Lewis put his eyeglasses on absentmindedly and waited, panting, his grin still radiating. It was almost pleasant to sit there on the ashy ground, gathering his breath and feeling, however temporarily, that his burden was shifting to someone else's shoulders. *It's not him. It's not him*, he sang inside.

"Your friend in the tutu has some interesting ideas about traitors," Boone mused after a long moment. "Something about German spies, was it?"

Lewis nodded, only half-hearing.

"Go on back to the car, Lewis. I'll be another few minutes. I want to take some pictures. And then…"

Lewis nodded again, absently. And then a bad thought emerged through his relief. Even if the body wasn't his dad, it was still somebody. Boone would have to report it, which meant police and questions and newspaper stories, and… maybe Child Services for two homeless children.

"And then what?" he repeated, looking up at Boone.

Boone gave Lewis a faint wink, seeming to understand what he was thinking. "There'll be no need to mention you two. Go on now. Wait in the car."

Lewis scrambled up and started off. He looked back once to see Boone moving toward the pit, camera in hand. Then Lewis faced forward. He didn't want to see what was buried there. He didn't want to be here.

Not anymore.

19

AN ENDLESS SUPPLY OF SLAG

By the time Lewis neared the car he was pretty sure he'd worked things out. Let Pearl regale the reporter with her treason story and explain all about her nefarious deed (which was just a general accusation, really, not an actual deed). He would put all his attention into figuring out where his dad had disappeared to.

Disappeared was so much better than dead. His dad was hiding, maybe, and if he was hiding, then maybe Lewis had bought him some time. After all, he had his dad's notebook and two of his dad's pots, and—Lewis was confident—Scrugg would have to search for him rather than his dad. He'd just lie low for a bit, not use the Flash. He'd had a huge breakfast, and cookies; it was a bellyful that could last him two days. And he had a dime in his pocket, and Pearl had one too.

Lewis felt as if his boots had springs in them, as if he were bouncing toward Boone's car. He'd give her the good news. Tell her they'd be fine.

But Pearl was not there. The Buick's driver-side door hung open, silent and dark.

Lewis turned, confused. Boone was still by the pit, the flash from his camera capturing the night. Lewis turned back, hands on hips, scanning the view. Trains rumbled and screeched in the distance, spilling their molten contents.

And then he saw her, standing on the rim opposite Boone, toward where the foul mist had long dissipated from the older, colder slag. A breeze had picked up, so her curls were tumbling in all directions and her tutu ruffled, sparkling in the faint glow.

Another wave of relief rushed over Lewis, taking him by surprise. When had that happened? When had not seeing Pearl become something worrisome? For Pete's sake. Lewis opened his mouth to call out and then closed it, not wanting to alert Boone. He trudged over to her instead, boots sloughing across the moonscape. Behind him another camera flash popped.

Pearl's hands were fashioned into a telescope, surveying the rim of the dump that circled farther off to the right. Lewis approached saying, "Hey—"

"This is a dump, isn't it?" she interrupted, as if he'd been beside her all along.

Same old Pearl. He needn't have felt even an ounce of worry. "Obviously," he answered.

"Then why are they loading up those train cars instead of emptying them?"

"Huh?"

Pearl pointed. Halfway across the rim a steam shovel labored, pouring great shovelfuls of cooled slag into three hoppers. "See? They're taking the garbage."

"Slag," Lewis corrected and shrugged. "Don't know why."

"Then we must go find out," said Pearl, and marched off. Lewis sighed. Yep. Same old Pearl.

He walked halfway around the great curve of the pit before catching up. She was crouched this time, studying the three hoppers that sat where a small section of tracks forked away from the main line. The fat steam shovel dug at the gravelly slag. An automobile sat just beyond the train cars, a Plymouth by its shape, and a clump of men huddled beside it in conversation. Lewis sat down next to Pearl and bent his head to catch his breath.

"What is Pickering and Lowe?" asked Pearl.

The name hit Lewis like a rock. He popped up. Sure

enough, bold black lettering ran across the sides of the hopper, huge and important looking. "Pickering and Lowe is the biggest steel company in the whole state," Lewis murmured, staring.

It was also the same company that had funded his father's recycling experiment. Lewis remembered how the company name was emblazoned on the fancy stationery sent to his dad announcing the awarding of a hundred-dollar stipend to Professor Harold Carter for the exploration of recycling P&L's deposits of heretofore unusable waste materials.

The steam shovel dropped its last load. After the hoppers were filled to bursting, the silhouettes of the men separated. Some climbed atop the railway cars and tightened canvases over the cargo. One figure stayed on the ground, pacing impatiently.

"Why would they want their slag back?" Pearl asked. "You said it was junk." Then, "Nigel? What is it?"

Lewis's hand shot out, pointing. The pacing figure had moved away from the shovel and rail cars, to where the orange glow outlined his shape. He was squat and wide, just like a bulldog.

"Mr. Scrugg!" Pearl gasped. "What's that traitor doing here?"

Lewis's hand stayed outstretched, his mind doing a terrible race. Ideas were all tumbling together like jigsaw pieces and falling into place.

"Nigel!" Pearl called him. "What's wrong? Nigel!"

"What if you're right?" He looked over at Pearl. "What if your aunt and Scrugg really do belong to a group who want to take over the United States and turn us all into Nazis?"

"The Nefarious Deed!" Pearl's eyes lit. "You believe me!"

"What would they need to take over a whole country?"

"An army. And weapons, of course," Pearl answered promptly.

A knot of menace was growing inside of Lewis. "And if

they wanted to win, then their weapons would have to be bigger and better than what our own army has, wouldn't it? Something that would take people by surprise or take them down quickly. Like the explosion at the watch repair shop." Lewis swallowed. "Only much, much worse."

He waited. Pearl's eyes were moon-sized, the light in them changing, as if they were reflecting the awfulness of his words. She whispered, "Where would they get so many weapons?"

"The slag." Lewis pointed at the hoppers again, and then gestured toward the enormous pit of waste. "That's what's in my father's notebook. He discovered how to make a weapon from recycled slag."

Lewis understood now why his father had gone so quiet, so secretive. It was an accident, not what he'd meant to find at all, and certainly his dad would never have shared deadly results with traitors. But they had found out anyway, and now they wanted his notes, his results. An endless supply of destruction.

There was a gasp from Pearl. "The hoppers are moving!"

Lewis snapped to attention. The railcars were grinding forward. Pearl and Lewis dived for the ground, watching from behind tufts of dead grass. The hoppers chugged past. Scrugg, silhouetted in the orange glow, watched them pull away. When they disappeared, he turned and climbed into the Plymouth. The taillights flashed on.

"He's leaving," Pearl cried, appalled. She leaped up in a swirl of pink and surged toward the Plymouth. Then she stopped dead, wheeled, and sprinted the other way, toward where Boone was still at work.

Lewis scrambled up and tore after Pearl. She was right: they should tell Boone what they'd just seen. Boone would know what to do.

The reporter was just visible in the orangey mist. He was digging, ankle deep in the slag, struggling with his shovel.

Pearl, racing, had nearly reached him. But then Pearl took a sharp turn when she should have stayed straight, running, not to Boone, but to his Buick. She flung herself through the open door into the driver's seat.

"What are you doing?" shouted Lewis.

She slammed the door and leaned out of the window. "Following Mr. Scrugg! Come on!"

"Hey!" Boone looked up at the shouting, and, seeing what was about to happen, began to clumsily climb out of the pit, waving his shovel in the air. "Stop! Hey!"

Pearl pulled her head back inside the car. There was a *vroom* and a screech and then the Buick lurched forward before sling-shotting back with a loud pop.

Lewis, catching up, flung open the passenger door. "You can't drive!" he gasped.

Pearl reached over and hauled Lewis in so hard that he catapulted over the seat and landed in the back, the passenger door flinging shut behind him.

"I am an *expert* at driving," she exclaimed. "Hang on!" Pearl yanked the clutch and wrenched the gear shift. There was another *vroom* and the Buick careened forward.

Lewis clawed himself upright just in time to be flung sideways as the Buick swerved onto the road. He got his knees on the seat and then his head bonked the rear window.

There, through the glass, receding in the distance, was Osgood Boone running after them, the beam of his flashlight sweeping wildly against the night sky.

20

PURSUIT

"Watch the curb! That's a stop sign! Don't hit the streetlamp!"

Lewis kept shouting warnings, as if that would keep them from flying into a spectacular crash. He could hardly believe what was happening. Pearl was driving.

Pearl was *driving!*

"I've got this," Pearl insisted between clenched teeth.

"How?" cried Lewis.

"Papa lets me drive his Speedster."

"When? You never see him—" Pearl's feet stamped on the brake and Lewis spluttered as they careened sideways, "For Pete's sake! Is your dad in the Demolition Derby?"

With a clunk, they were on four wheels again and, luckily, a straightaway. Pearl took what sounded like her first breath, though her hands still throttled the steering wheel. "Movie stars drive Speedsters," she announced. "Errol Flynn drives a Speedster, I'll have you know."

"I'm coming up front." Lewis poured himself into the passenger seat, planted his feet on the floorboard for leverage, then gasped. Pearl's eyeballs were barely level with the top of the dashboard. How could she see? "Of all the loony ideas you've had, this—!"

"We're in this together, Nigel, so compose yourself!"

Compose? Lewis would laugh if he had any breath. Except—Pearl was right. She might have jumped first, but he was right beside her, stealing a car, no less. And chasing a man who—if Lewis had this figured out—was trying to build bombs. Despite how utterly crazy all of this was, he couldn't deny the excitement stirring inside of him. He was excited. In fact, he was thrilled.

"He's turning! Here we go!" There was a shriek of rubber as Pearl violently yanked the wheel. Scrugg's taillights made a sharp left. Pearl turned, too, but straight into the path of an oncoming vehicle. Lewis yelped as Pearl swerved back, leaving an inch between them to spare. She slammed on the brake and blasted the horn. The other driver slid past them, his face white with terror.

"How dare he!" Pearl cried, furious, shaking her fist. "He ruined it! I missed the turn! Mr. Scrugg's gone!"

"Go back!" Lewis said urgently. He was fully in it now.

There was the slightest pause. Pearl gulped, "I don't know how to reverse!"

This wasn't the time to crow at Pearl's admission, finally, of *not* knowing something. "Gas," he barked.

"What?"

"Gas. Now!"

Pearl shifted the gear, floored the gas pedal, and Lewis leaned over, grabbing hold of the steering wheel and dragging it toward him. The Buick squealed, circled up and over the curb, skidded across some frozen grass, and plopped back down in the road.

"Take it!"

Pearl grabbed the wheel. "That was amazing," she exclaimed, aiming for the missed turn. Lewis put his hands on the dashboard and tried to breathe.

Now they were on a smaller, less traveled road, bordered by disheveled garages and scrubby lots. It wound on for a while, the two of them silent, Pearl's fingers white-clenched on the wheel, Lewis barely breathing. Then up ahead, in the distance, they could see a new glow: not the orange cauldron of Brown's Dump, but a whiter glow, like a halo of light illuminating clouds of smoke.

"What is that?" whispered Lewis, awed.

"A hideout," Pearl answered decisively. "He's heading there. That's what villains do."

They rumbled forward, following the pinpricks of Scrugg's taillights. The road changed from asphalt to dirt. And now there were row houses, lined up in grim formation, sharing laundry lines and front yards.

"Do you hear that?" Pearl asked, as they thunked over a particularly deep rut in the uneven road.

Lewis listened. Above the engine noise came a new sound, like rushing water but hollower somehow. "Sounds like machinery."

"Ooh, never mind! He's turning!" The glint of red taillights suddenly disappeared. "It's a shortcut!"

"Careful," cautioned Lewis as Pearl jammed her foot on the gas. "It's really dark."

"I can see!" she cried.

But apparently, she couldn't. Pearl turned too soon, and they vaulted from the path onto a rubbish-strewn lot and for a moment they were zooming forward and then there was a bump and a large bang and the Buick suddenly stopped, listing badly to the right.

"Tire," wailed Pearl.

She looked at Lewis, Lewis looked at her, and then they burst out of the Buick, slamming the doors and racing after the disappeared taillights. They tore across the lot, which was an obstacle course of rusted things. A dog began barking madly.

"Where did he go?" shouted Lewis. His chest was heaving so hard there were spots in front of his eyes.

"There!" cried Pearl. She pointed behind the houses, where a narrow, unpaved path could be seen.

Pearl and Lewis charged through a gap between two houses and onto the path. Luckily, Scrugg's auto had slowed to crawl down an icy hill. They were able to gain on him, stopping, finally, at the hill's crest. There they had a stunning view of where the road ended, and of where the roaring noise and glow had come from.

Nine smokestacks, like the spines of some iron behemoth, belched ribbons of black soot into the night sky. At their base, giant searchlights blazed, illuminating the smoke and soggy night and great tangles of machinery pipes and tubing. A few narrow buildings were jammed behind the smokestacks, and beyond that there were train tracks, then a steep drop into the churning Monongahela River. Across the river was more of the same—a second confusion of buildings and searchlights and billowing smoke.

"Some hideout!" breathed Pearl while Lewis crouched, wheezing. "It's a fortress!"

It did look like a fortress—huge and forbidding. But something else had caught Lewis's eye. Slowly he stood up. Underneath all the wheezing, his lungs started to fizz.

In gigantic letters, printed down the sides of the smokestacks and sculpted along the curve of a wrought-iron sign arching over the main entrance, was the name:

Pickering & Lowe Steel

"Look! There's Mr. Scrugg!" cried Pearl, as the Plymouth rumbled beneath the entryway arch straight into the plant. "Come on!"

A long, steep staircase was built into the side of the hill for steelworkers to get from their row houses to the factory. They ducked under the railings and clattered down the rickety steps.

Lewis couldn't match Pearl's speed. "Go on!" he gasped. "I'll catch up."

Pearl nodded and flew ahead. Lewis paused to drag in air that tasted like metal shavings, hating his stupid lungs with every wasted second.

He dodged the gatehouse attendant, crawled under a bar at the entrance, then limped on toward the river—beneath the arch, beneath towering furnaces, past enormous drums and vats, trucks and barrels and pipes, all while avoiding soot-smeared workers. Furnaces roared like thunder and the air crackled with heat, splitting the frosty night and searing his nose and the back of his throat.

At the waterfront, Lewis stopped to suck in deep, ugly breaths. The clash of hot and cold air created a cloying fog along the bank, and he could barely see anything. Did Scrugg work here? Was this steel company how his dad had gotten mixed up with traitors?

"Nigel!"

Lewis turned his head. Farther up the bank, like a butterfly fluttering in the haze, was Pearl. She was pointing to the river, where lights glowed through the fog. Lewis squinted. He saw a barge ferrying equipment to the other half of the steel plant. On it was the Plymouth, with the bulldog leaning against the driver's door, arms folded across his chest. Lewis just gaped. Scrugg was going—he was gone.

He trudged over to Pearl, said furiously, "If I weren't so slow, we'd be on that barge." Then, "I'm sorry."

Pearl scoffed. "Don't be silly, Nigel. It's not as if we could have snuck onto it." She nodded at the barge. "No place to hide."

"But we should have had a plan, like you said—"

"Oh, pooh," Pearl dismissed. "Lola and Nigel rarely have a plan, they work on instinct—well, Lola does, because she's so brave. Nigel is…"

She seemed to decide it was better to leave Nigel's role unsaid and Lewis had to laugh. A little. "Gee. Thanks."

Two workers appeared out of the fog, sharing a cigarette. "We should move," Lewis urged. And so they picked their way along the steep river edge, avoiding the spots where factory muck was leaching into the water and trying not to look at the glow from the opposite bank that beckoned, tantalizing and impossible.

It was Pearl who broke the silence.

"I want to say how pleased I am that your father is not decomposing in the dump."

In all the hullaballoo, he'd completely forgotten. Lewis smiled. "Mr. Boone found a Nazi medallion, which my dad would never own." He described the eagle, its claw clutching the swastika.

"Aunt Gimlick has that very same medallion pinned to the inside of her coat," said Pearl. "I bet all the traitors wear them, so they can identify each other!"

"I don't get it. Your aunt isn't struggling like everyone. What could she hate about our country that makes her think Nazis would be better?"

"She likes how Hitler wants everything to be in order. Everyone to be like her."

"My dad would say order ruins imagination."

"Order is evil," said Pearl flatly. "At least the way Aunt Gimlick insists on it." She added after a moment, "Papa laughs that Hitler is just a puny bully pretending he's powerful. But Papa doesn't believe anyone can truly be evil."

That explained why Pearl's eccentric father didn't seem to understand that Aunt Gimlick was so mean. "Hitler's building an army," Lewis said, remembering the headlines. "What if he really plans to take over the world?"

"And these traitors are trying to help him." Pearl stepped toward Lewis then, her gaze and voice determined. "We're the only ones who know about the Nefarious Deed and your father's experiment, so we're the ones who *have* to stop them."

"Sure. If we could just find—" Lewis froze, staring ahead at the river. "That's it!" He grabbed Pearl's sleeve. "The Hot Metal Bridge!"

"The what?"

Lewis pointed at an ominous-looking apparition that had just emerged from the fog—a great web of iron trusses and stone piers stretching high above the river. "The Hot—oh, the bridge isn't hot," Lewis clarified, his heart lifting. "It's a railroad bridge. See?" A set of open-topped gondola cars began a slow trek across the bridge just then, spitting red sparks as they traveled. "Those cars are carrying molten pig iron from this side of the river to the furnaces on the other."

"Is it the same as what's at the dump?" Pearl asked.

"No. Pig iron's not the waste, it's what becomes steel!" Lewis laughed. "And anyway, who cares? That's our way across!"

Minutes later he and Pearl confronted the span of tracks, with troughs and metal plates all jimmied together to keep the hot iron from spraying into the churning river below. A stiff breeze gusted up from the dark water. They waited for a train to pass, in a swirl of steam and sparks, the steel workers hanging between the cars, looking like ghouls with the whites of their eyes glowing in soot-rimed faces.

"Get off the bridge, you kids!" the men shouted. "You'll get yourselves killed!"

Lewis only grinned, feeling as undaunted and cheeky as Mac or Duck. "Ready?" he called over the shriek of wheels and wind. Pearl nodded.

He looked at her for just an extra moment. Pearl, in all her silly pinkness, her tutu dancing in the wind. "Pearl Alice Clavell," he burst out sort of gallantly, "you're the bravest girl I know."

Pearl lit up like a beacon. "Really?"

"Promise." He didn't exactly know any other girls, but Lewis still thought Pearl would be the bravest.

"Of course I am," said Pearl, and she tossed her curls.

21

INTO THE FORTRESS

The northern side of the Pickering & Lowe steel plant was even more enormous than the southern. There were fewer smokestacks, but the buildings were bigger and longer. There was more activity too. Even at this hour, workers were everywhere, too busy to notice streeters.

Lewis and Pearl crept in the shadows until they spied Scrugg's Plymouth parked between a huge brick building and some train tracks, on which sat three hoppers with Pickering & Lowe printed along their sides. Though every train car and vehicle here was boldly painted with the company's name, these hoppers were lashed with canvas and rope, just like the ones at Brown's Dump.

They looked at each other. Then Pearl abruptly mimed *stay here* and darted across the cold, gray lot. She climbed one of the hoppers and slipped a hand under the canvas, then vaulted down and raced back. With a triumphant smile, Pearl held up her hand. It was gray with dead-looking grit and sludge. "Slag," Lewis confirmed.

"What next?" Pearl asked, wiping her hand on her tutu.

"Let's get inside that building," Lewis answered. "Come on!"

A minute later Pearl and Lewis were hunkered at the entrance of the brick building, behind an upended wheelbarrow, staring open-mouthed. It was a furnace house, huge and stifling hot, with a cacophony of hissing steam, roaring fire, clanging metal, and shouting workers. Huge tanks of molten steel towered along one side, spilling into a giant vat, billowing sparks and steam. High above, beams, pipes, and catwalks crisscrossed every which way. Men stood precariously upon them, wrestling huge pulleys and chains, yelling to each other above the din, avoiding the flames and the viciously spitting steel. Lewis couldn't imagine working as they did when the very air seared his lungs.

He swallowed and scoured the space. Big as it was, there wasn't room for those hoppers to deliver the slag, or any sort of spot where they might refine it.

Pearl elbowed his ribs. "Scrugg, ten o'clock!"

There, on the far side of a giant column, the bulldog was clomping toward the back, where there was a row of makeshift offices with doors and walls but no ceilings. The bulldog pulled up short, tugged at his collar, then opened a door and shut it behind him. His squat silhouette filled the mottled glass window, and his arms began to wave up and down emphatically.

"He's talking! Someone else is in there!" Pearl cried. "We have to see who it is!"

Behind some barrels, Lewis spied a metal ladder stretching up to the catwalks. He prodded Pearl and pointed, and they scurried to it and climbed, hardly bothering to be quiet since the roaring was so loud and the men so focused. Once up, Lewis held the walkway's thin wire railings and Pearl held Lewis. They moved in tandem until they got as close to Scrugg's room as they dared. Lewis dropped to his belly, panting, and peered down. Pearl lowered herself beside him.

A network of pipes obstructed much of the view, but Lewis could see the corner of a desk and the side of a filing cabinet. He could see the top of Scrugg's greasy head and the shoulders of his ugly green suit. There were two pairs of feet as well, a man's and a woman's. The woman wore high-heeled boots trimmed with fur. The man's black shoes gleamed, like they'd never touched snow or mud. His trouser hems were crisply pleated, and the visible bit of his wool coat looked brand new and very warm. He was seated, hands resting on the chair arms. On his pinkie finger was a gold signet ring.

"Crusts," Lewis muttered.

Scrugg paced in front of the pair, nervous and overly loud. His voice carried straight up. "I don't see the problem. Smolpenski got a brain, he don't need no fancy instructions. He can hire another scientist guy, like the last one."

Lewis gasped, and Pearl's hand shot out to grip his arm.

Scrugg then burst out, "I said I got my best men lookin'! It don't mean the load can't go tonight!"

"Go? Without the—? Oh, honestly, what is this dolt paid for?" the woman snapped. It was Aunt Gimlick.

Lewis glanced at Pearl. Fears for his dad were bad enough, but this proved Aunt Gimlick was involved. Pearl's face was lit by the roaring furnaces and emotions flickered across it like flames—shock, anger, exultation. He wondered: if they caught Aunt Gimlick in some sort of treasonous espionage, could the snake be sent to jail? Then what would happen to Pearl?

Below, the seated man said, "Quiet, or you'll wait in the car, Matilda."

Pearl turned to Lewis. It was the booming voice from the phone at the jeweler's shop. "The evil boss," she mouthed, and Lewis nodded.

The boss now spoke, slowly and menacingly to Scrugg: "Our colleagues expect the material and instructions at the designated time. Your job is to facilitate that delivery."

Scrugg was bobbing his head in agreement. "I know, I know." Beads of sweat had popped out on his broad neck above his ugly green collar.

"And I think, Floyd," the boss continued, his ring glinting sharply as he squeezed the chair arm, "you understand the consequences of failure. To you, personally."

The threat was clear in that hard, pompous tone. "I'll get 'em." Scrugg promised, nodding so violently it looked like his head might fall off. "I'll get 'em."

The boss made an impatient move. One hand disappeared, then returned, clenching a pair of leather gloves. He slapped them against his knee.

"Yes, you will," he said, then stood. Lewis could see only the back of the boss's head and his thick silvery hair as he bent to don a fedora. He straightened, imposingly tall and broad, and strode from sight with Aunt Gimlick clack-clacking after him. There was a slamming of the door and Pearl and Lewis rolled to look the other way, but they couldn't see.

Pearl tugged at Lewis's jacket. "The evil boss looks very rich! No wonder Aunt Gimlick kowtows to him!"

Lewis nodded, then scrunched his eyes and clenched his teeth. He wouldn't let his worry about the notebook and his father undo him. Not here, not now. Lewis forced himself to look back down at the office where Scrugg was shifting his weight from side to side as if he didn't know which way to go. Then, abruptly, the bulldog bolted out of the office, slamming the door behind him.

Lewis pushed himself over the edge of the catwalk, hung so his toes touched one of the pipes, then worked himself to a large enough gap where he could drop into the office and onto the desk. He set himself onto the floor with a cough. Pearl followed silently, landing in a flutter of tulle.

"What are we going to do?" she whispered.

Lewis looked around. The desk was strewn with ashtrays and crumpled cigarette packets and a keychain with a horseshoe on it. There were smears of liverwurst and dried crumbs from old sandwiches and a used pair of socks. He opened the desk drawer, which held more crumbs and more stinky socks. Scrugg was the worst kind of slob—no wonder Aunt Gimlick hated him.

Lewis pushed the drawer shut and answered Pearl. "There has to be something here that will tell us what they're planning with those hoppers of slag."

"You already said what they're planning," said Pearl.

"They're going to refine it into weapons, using the code from your father's notebook—"

"Yes, but something that shows how they'll do it," Lewis revised impatiently, feeling his ideas were vague and unhelpful. "We have to find proof."

"Okay," said Pearl.

She dropped to her knees and began tapping the floorboards and listening. Lewis opened his mouth to say how silly that looked, like she was expecting to find Nazis hiding under the floor or something.

But he didn't. Because when he ditched Pearl at North Market, she hadn't gotten angry. When he said the Nefarious Deed and his father's experiment were connected, she hadn't rolled her eyes or held him back or told him he was crazy. Nor had she argued when he'd said to find something. She'd simply said okay. Pearl trusted him—she hardly knew Lewis, yet she trusted him.

It was time for him to start trusting her.

Oblivious to his thoughts, Pearl continued tapping the floorboards. "Secrets are never in the open, Nigel," she cried. "Look for hiding places!"

Lewis stared at her, then turned to the wooden filing cabinet and tugged the handles. "Locked," he muttered and kicked it for good measure. Pearl hopped up and withdrew the bobby pin that had held her bow in place for the past two days. In a heartbeat, the cabinet drawers were open.

Inside the drawers was a heap of disorganized garbage: ripped-up pamphlets, a list of employee salaries, charts of steel prices and foreign tariffs, and old ticket stubs. Behind all this trash was an empty carton. Lewis pulled it out to read the label.

"Bullets," he said grimly, and tossed the box back in. He pulled out the one non-torn-up pamphlet.

"What's that?" Pearl asked.

"Railroad timetable." He opened it, Pearl reading over his

shoulder. The schedule was for trains departing from Pennsylvania Station. The 11:30 p.m. to Buffalo time slot was circled. "What's in Buffalo?" he wondered aloud.

"More Nazis," Pearl said in distaste. "Aunt Gimlick gets correspondence from Buffalo."

"What kind of correspondence?"

"Letters, donation pamphlets, newsletters…all from the Friends of New Germany—" Pearl's eyes widened. "The coded messages! What if they're sending the slag to Buffalo?"

"That could explain why the hoppers are here but not unloaded," ventured Lewis. "But why send it so far away?" His mind churned, picturing the shape of New York State and where exactly Buffalo was. Something hovered at the edge of his understanding. If only he could reach out and grab it.

"Buffalo would be a perfect place to hide something this big," said Pearl. She went dreamy. "They could float it all, on a great houseboat in the middle of Lake Erie, under cover of darkness with little signal lights—"

"Pearl!" Lewis shouted. "That's it!"

"The great houseboat—?"

"No! Erie! Not Lake Erie, but the Erie Canal! It starts in Buffalo! It's like a gateway to…to everywhere!"

Pearl gasped, then exploded, "The canal! Nigel, that's brilliant!"

It was. The great canal funneled goods by barge between Buffalo and Albany, where the goods could travel farther south via the Hudson River and far beyond.

Pearl's eyes were now as wide as saucers. She said breathlessly, "This is bigger than *anything* Lola Lavender has ever solved!"

Lewis exhaled in a mix of triumph and disbelief. A beautiful smile spread across Pearl's face. Maybe they hadn't figured it all out, but they'd figured out something. They. Together. He smiled back.

Just then, there was the horrible, terrifying noise of a key in a lock. The office door flew open, and the bulldog's huge frame filled the entrance.

"Well, well. Lookee here," sneered Scrugg. "Jes' heard a couple of kids were pokin' round tonight. And whaddaya know? Here they are."

The train schedule flew out of Lewis's hand as Pearl shoved him hard.

"Run!" she screamed.

22

BARTERING

Lewis staggered sideways. Pearl jumped on the desk and leaped at Scrugg, who stumbled back, his arms windmilling.

"*Run!*" Pearl screamed again, tugging Scrugg's ears with all her might.

Lewis found his feet and dashed around Scrugg. "Pearl, come on!" he shouted, then tore down the corridor. The office doors were lined up on the right; to the left was the cavernous space, filled with equipment and supplies, all licked by the glare from the furnace. Panting, he flung himself sideways behind some barrels of machine grease. They were still at it, Scrugg thrashing about while Pearl twisted his ears. When the bulldog's hands finally went to grab her, she pushed off and went sprinting out the door.

"Pearl!" Lewis hissed as she neared. "Pearl!" But Pearl couldn't hear him over the roar of machinery and ran right past, toward the entrance, toward the showers of sparks and heat and molten steel. Scrugg pounded behind, rubbing his ears, a mean look on his ugly mug. Lewis tagged after, keeping to the shadows. The steel workers were ahead, manning the furnace. Lewis couldn't imagine Scrugg would dare do anything in front of them.

But Scrugg was already shouting to one, his voice carrying with deafening force. "Hey! You there, Harding! Grab that kid!"

To Lewis's horror, one of the soot-grimed workers reached out and deftly hooked Pearl in mid-stride. Pearl went pinwheeling, but the man, Harding, was strong—he walked the flailing girl back to Scrugg. Pearl immediately kicked

Scrugg in the shin, and Scrugg yanked her by the arm. "Ruffian!" he growled down at her.

"Traitor!" she screamed in return.

The worker seemed taken aback by Scrugg's behavior. "H—hey now," he stuttered anxiously. "She didn't do any harm that I saw, Mr. Scrugg. No harm. But kids shouldn't be around here. You either. Could get yourself killed in a splash of steel."

"You have to help!" Pearl cried to the worker. "He's selling secrets to Hitler! He's going to *murder* us!"

Lewis was aghast. The bulldog's face had gone all red. His fist was tightening around Pearl's elbow. "Heh, heh," he barked stiffly. "These streeters'll tell ya a mouthful of lies fer a penny, right, Harding?"

Harding now looked extremely uncomfortable. He scratched an ear.

Go on, Pearl, Lewis urged silently. *Do your movie star thing. Bat your eyelashes, look tearful. Something!*

But Pearl wasn't doing anything of the sort. She struggled against Scrugg's grip, wild, trying to stamp his feet.

"You did good, Harding. Mighty good," Scrugg soothed as the man's worried eyes fixed on Pearl. "Look how crazy this one is! She coulda—"

All three ducked as, with an extra violent roar, a spray of red-gold molten steel shot into the air.

"No sirree," Scrugg continued, straightening. "Don't want no kids gettin' hurt 'round here, right? That'd bring in all sorts of inspections—could shut down the factory, why, you'd lose your *job*. But you saved us, Harding. Bet you'll get a monetary reward." Scrugg nodded hard, as if to confirm it. "Yep. In fact, there's another streeter scuttlin' around here. If ya spot him, grab him. I'll make sure that reward is doubled."

That put an end to any of Harding's misgivings. The worker turned once more toward the harshly blazing furnace without another word, his eyes darting in several directions, as though he had every intention of finding the other streeter. Scrugg turned and marched a shouting Pearl back to the office, with Lewis following like a shadow and slipping once more behind the barrels of grease. He watched as the bulldog tossed Pearl inside the office and slammed the door shut, at which point the doorknob began rattling so furiously Scrugg had to hold it with both hands and couldn't reach for his key.

Scrugg turned around, holding the doorknob fast behind him, his great body blocking the door. "You're here somewhere, Lewis Carter," he bellowed, well over the din of the furnace.

"No, he isn't!!" yelled Pearl.

Lewis scrunched down. His hands went to his jacket side pockets by reflex, then he pulled them back. What was he thinking? He couldn't use the Flash so close to these flammable supplies.

Scrugg called louder over the roar. "Seems to me we been here before, Lewis. You hidin' an' me lookin', remember?"

Lewis remembered: the alley and the fire escape and Scrugg angrily turning over all the garbage cans.

"So," Scrugg called, "let's barter, like last time. Yer friend fer the notebook."

"Absolutely not!" yelled Pearl from behind the door.

Scrugg kicked the door with his heel in response. "She's feisty, ain't she?"

"And you, Mr. Scrugg, are an evil spy!" came through the door. Lewis winced as Scrugg kicked the door again so hard it gave a sharp *crack!*

"I'm waitin', Lewis!" he shouted. "'Cuz if ya don't barter, then I'll figger out somethin' else to do with this snitch. Something good and perm-a-nent. Might jes' drop her in one of them vats of molten steel." The bulldog chuckled then, like he approved of his own idea. Lewis's hands clenched into fists. "Yep. Quick an' tidy."

Lewis's knuckles were white. Would Scrugg do that? Was

Scrugg so evil he would actually drop Pearl into molten steel?

"Can't think that little bitty notebook means more than the ballerina here."

"It does, Nigel! Don't make any deal!" Pearl rattled the door wildly.

"Shaddap!" barked Scrugg and kicked the door so hard the hinges bulged. But Pearl didn't shut up. She kept taunting and the bulldog grew more and more frustrated; as if anger was expanding that ugly green suit. Yet he didn't move, and it seemed after a bit that maybe Pearl was right. That Scrugg didn't dare throw her into a vat of boiling metal.

But then, with a gulp that dropped like a stone into the pit of his stomach, Lewis realized that Scrugg wasn't hesitating. He was waiting. And who he was waiting for had just arrived.

"Lazy oaf! You won't find the professor's notebook by standing here!" Aunt Gimlick came clacking up the corridor, maneuvering around oil stains and metal droppings.

Scrugg looked relieved, though he answered lazily enough. "Must make you sore, Tildy. The boss'll never need you as much as he needs me. An' I barely have to lift a finger."

"I'm indispensable to the cause," Aunt Gimlick snorted derisively. "You're a filthy thug."

"Aww, I should take offense. But I'm a nice guy." Scrugg jerked a thumb at the office behind him. "In fact, I got a gift fer ya." He gave an insolent grin and went to turn the doorknob, but it didn't budge. Aunt Gimlick snorted again.

Reddening, the bulldog cursed and heaved his whole body at the door, then went flying inwards. Lewis craned his neck to see. There was a scuffle and an *oof*, and then Scrugg grunted, "Look who's come home, Tildy."

Aunt Gimlick teetered to the doorway and shrieked. "Why you little miscreant!"

"Stay away from me!" Pearl shouted.

"How could you? Running off like that!" Gimlick's voice was shrill. "What would your father say?"

"Don't you *dare* talk about Papa!" cried Pearl.

Lewis's heart was pounding, his lungs fizzing. He was trying desperately to see Pearl, who was trapped behind her aunt. There was a tremor in Pearl's voice he'd never heard before.

"Dare? My, such rudeness!" sniffed Aunt Gimlick.

"That's two of 'em bein' rude." Scrugg had huffed himself upright and was helping Gimlick block the doorway. "Yer niece's friend is skulkin' 'round here somewhere. Pretty sure he knows where to find the notebook"—Scrugg twisted his neck and yelled out to the cavernous space—"that he *stole.*" He swiveled back. "But ya know he don't seem to be budging much. So I was jes' recallin' the meltin' properties of hot steel when you showed up."

"Really," Aunt Gimlick said with interest.

There was a look, Lewis saw, that went between the snake and the bulldog, and then Gimlick's hand went to her chest. This time when she spoke, she turned her head so Lewis could hear every chilling word quite clearly: "I see your point, Floyd. Naughty children must be taught to obey their elders."

There was a fumbling in the doorway and Pearl appeared between the grown-ups. Scrugg had her firmly by one arm, and Gimlick clutched a handful of Pearl's curls. "A rat's nest!" she seethed, yanking. Pearl's face screwed up tightly and her lips pressed into a thin line.

"Let's go," ordered Scrugg, pushing Pearl in front of them. "Say goodbye."

That was all he could bear. Lewis flung himself from the barrels straight into their path. "Stop!" he ordered.

Gimlick jumped. Pearl's eyes sprang open. "Nigel! No!"

But Scrugg grinned—wide enough so his gold tooth glinted. "Well now. If it ain't the professor's son."

"Let her go," Lewis demanded, squaring his shoulders. "Let her go and you can have the notebook."

"Yeah?" Scrugg sneered gleefully.

"He doesn't have it!" Pearl raged. "Get out, Nigel, now!" She aimed her foot again at Scrugg's shin but was viciously yanked back by her aunt.

"Give it here." Scrugg took a step forward, holding out a beefy paw.

"No!" Pearl cried.

Lewis dug inside his jacket for his father's precious notes. There were a thousand echoes of *No!* in his head, but the bigger shout was *Hurry!* He pulled out the little red notebook and held it up, his hand steady, though his insides were a riot of fizz and rapid heartbeats.

Scrugg's smile could not get uglier. It spread across his face. "Would ya look at that, Tildy. Guess I'm not so lazy, eh?"

Aunt Gimlick licked her lips at the sight of the notebook.

"Let Pearl go first," Lewis spat.

"Nah. Miss Imp here'll just run, an' then you'll run, an' that wouldn't be fair, would it? You first."

Lewis looked back and forth between the grown-ups and Pearl. Pearl shook her head as best she could under Gimlick's grip, but the aunt held Pearl's curls fast in her hand, looking almost disappointed she wouldn't be dispatching her niece in a vat of steel.

Pearl's aunt turned his stomach. She was cruel. So was Scrugg. But he could beat them, Lewis was certain. Once he and Pearl got out of here, they could find Boone—at the paper maybe, or with Dwight's help. They'd tell the reporter everything about the slag and what the traitors were planning. They could do all that and still have time to stop the 11:30 to Buffalo.

And even if they couldn't stop it, any of it, the most important thing was Pearl. Pearl, with her loony ideas and awful karate chops and irritatingly pink fluffy-ness, was not going back with Gimlick, not if he could help it.

He gripped the notebook tighter. "Fair's fair," he answered firmly. "We'll do it at the same time."

"Well now, kid," said Scrugg, his mouth peeling wide. "That's how you barter."

"No!" Pearl begged. "Don't!"

Lewis cleared his throat. "Okay. On three. One." He edged the tiniest bit closer. "Two—"

"So honest," smirked Scrugg, reaching. "Jes' like the professor."

The mention of his father caught Lewis off guard. He wavered—just a tiny waver, but Scrugg was on him. It happened so fast Lewis barely got a breath out, but then he was shouting and Pearl was screaming and Scrugg had the notebook in one hand and Lewis in the other.

Lewis flailed, vainly trying to free himself from Scrugg's grip. Pearl was flailing too, but Aunt Gimlick's red-painted claws had dug into Pearl's shoulders, keeping her in place.

"You double crosser!" Lewis yelled at them. "You got what you need! Let us go!"

Scrugg laughed. Then he yanked Lewis closer and bent down to hiss, "Notebook? Heck, the notebook's no use without someone to interpret all them crazy, gibberish notes."

A trill of sheer terror ran down Lewis's spine. "What do you mean?"

Scrugg's grip tightened like a metal vice. "I mean, we need *you*, Lewis Carter. And we ain't losin' you this time."

"No. No!" Lewis redoubled his efforts, shouting, his arms and legs going every which way. Pearl was hollering even louder. He wished a worker from up front would hear them above the roaring furnace.

"Enough." Scrugg stuck the notebook in the breast pocket of his ugly green suit, then whisked something else from a side pocket. It was that oily, horrid-smelling cloth he'd used before. Lewis gasped one warning, "Pearl!" just before Scrugg pushed the cloth over his nose and he couldn't speak or breathe.

The world started to go fuzzy. There was a flurry of bodies brushing by—Pearl, he thought. Was she attacking Aunt Gimlick? How extraordinary: Pearl was biting Gimlick's hand and Gimlick was bouncing up and down like a jumping bean, not a snake, screaming, "She's getting away!"

"Go, Pearl. Go," he mumbled, willing her to safety. And then it was too hard to do anything at all.

Lewis closed his eyes.

23

ELEVEN-THIRTY TO BUFFALO

Stupid, bumpy trolley, Lewis thought crossly. Everything was jostling up, down, and sideways, making his head all woozy. He should have skipped the fare and walked. He should, Lewis repeated, insisting...except he couldn't seem to make himself get up.

There was another jolt, another bump, and suddenly something about this felt familiar—horribly familiar—about trolleys, and saving a nickel, and not really being on a trolley but—

With a groan, Lewis cracked open one eyelid. He knew exactly what was so horrible. He'd been kidnapped. Again. His hands and feet were tied again, and he was probably upside down under Scrugg's arm, again. He grimaced, popping open the other eye. A ceiling blinked into view, all shiny like enamel, with glowing light bulbs spaced neatly along it. Lewis struggled up. He wasn't under Scrugg's arm, but on a train, on a scratchy upholstered seat, near the middle of a passenger carriage. The train was creeping slowly, lurching over each little weld of track.

Lewis spun to the windows. It was night. And they were in Pittsburgh, he could tell. To his left Liberty Avenue stretched out under pools of streetlights. Across on his right was the steep ridge that paralleled Liberty's southern edge. They were downtown still, barely out of Pennsylvania Station. Lewis twisted, squinting through the pane of glass in the carriage's back entry. He couldn't see much, except portions of the canvas-lashed Pickering & Lowe hoppers, rocking behind in a tail.

The 11:30 to Buffalo.

Lewis turned slowly back and sank against the seat. He shook his head to clear it, which only made his eyeglasses slip.

A chorus of laughs erupted from the front of his train car. Lewis nudged his glasses into place using the seat in front of him and peered over its top. Near the head of the car sat three burlies. Massive, muscled, murderous-looking burlies, all sprawled in seats, going for the ride. Lewis recognized two of them from the restaurant. The rest of the seats were empty. No other passenger was on the train.

Except for Scrugg. He stood at the very front of the car, leaning through the open door between carriages and talking at the engineer—yelling, really—something about not getting to Buffalo until next year at this speed. The engineer yelled back that they wouldn't get to Buffalo at all if they spilled any slag on the city tracks.

Lewis slumped. One passenger car and three hoppers. Three burlies and Scrugg. Slag…and Nazis. What he wouldn't give to be back at Knoertzer's Grocery, pinching sausages. But it wasn't sausages he suddenly pictured, it was Pearl, and worry darted through his thoughts. Had she escaped? Or did Aunt Gimlick have her scissors out, snipping at Pearl's scalp while gloating over her grand scheme for arming traitors?

Lewis sat up. He wasn't any good to Pearl *or* his dad trapped in a train car. He had to get out, *now*, before the train picked up speed.

He shifted, feeling his way around his binds. This was good—he wasn't tied to anything. Lewis slid to the floor and squeezed between the seats to the aisle. He hunched over to make himself as small as possible, then shifted one knee forward an inch, then the other, as quietly as he could. A hundred more inches like this, he calculated.

He made it about three feet.

"Lookee, boys! The little slug's wormin' along back there!"

Scrugg clomped down the aisle, lifted Lewis by his jacket,

and tossed him right back in the seat, then hung over him, grinning that hideous grin, his squat frame filling the space and sucking away all the air. Lewis said savagely, "Get back, will you? I can't breathe so well."

Scrugg snorted but stepped back and dropped into the opposite seat. "Shufflin' off on yer—Hey!" he shouted to the burlies. "'Shuffle Off to Buffalo,' get it?" The burlies laughed as if that were the funniest thing they'd ever heard and Scrugg seemed so pleased with his joke that he offered Lewis a compliment. "Gotta say, kid. Yer a fighter. Like me!"

Lewis struggled upright and fixed the bulldog with a glare of loathing. "I'm nothing like you. Where's Pearl?"

"Ah, don't worry 'bout Miss Imp. She's safe at home with her auntie."

"Snake, you mean."

Scrugg chuckled. "You an' me agree about that."

Lewis deflated inside. Pearl…poor Pearl. He scowled at Scrugg. "It doesn't matter. She won't be there long. We know what you're trying to do, so you may as well give up now."

Scrugg chuckled on, unconcerned. "Yeah? I'm quakin' in my boots. Hold on so's I can tell the engineer to turn around."

"You're fixing to arm Nazi supporters here with weapons!" Lewis accused in the loudest voice he could. When no burly reacted and Scrugg just kept chuckling, he bit out, "What's in this for you? Why are you helping Nazis?"

Scrugg's chuckle faded. "Work's work," he spat. "Don't waste time wonderin' whut for."

He'd hit a nerve with the bulldog. Lewis dug in. He wanted to keep the bulldog talking, wanted to learn everything he could about their plans while he figured out a better way to escape. "Guess you do all the boss's dirty work because he says so, huh? Real dedicated, aren't you—getting paid to kidnap kids and be a traitor!"

"Watch yer mouth, kid."

Lewis ignored the threat. "How'd you find me, anyway? That night, after the grocery. How'd you find me? Boss tell you where to go?"

That seemed to hit another nerve, a different sort of nerve, for Scrugg peered skyward, a smug little grin spreading across his face. "Yer wrong. That was all me."

"Yeah, sure it was," baited Lewis.

Scrugg bit. "I'll tell ya how. We knew the Flash Gang was using your dad's experiment to make them special flashes, an' the boss was none too pleased someone was usin' up material that belonged to him, and gettin' famous on it, no less. So he asked me to make certain the professor hadn't sold his secrets to somebody else."

"My dad's experiment doesn't belong to your stupid boss."

Scrugg ignored that, grinning wider. "Got a friend or two on the police force, ya might say. Give 'em a checker an' they alert me to any Flash Gang doings. I'd hoof it to each spot, lookin' for signs of who mighta set 'em."

"It's a gang," Lewis said, unwilling to admit his role. "Fat Joe's mob."

Scrugg laughed out loud and turned to look straight at Lewis. "Think yer so smart, kid? I'm smarter." He jerked at thumb at his chest. "I pay attention, see? The mob ain't involved, an' I'll tell ya why: what does the Flash Gang take? Food. Where'd some of that food show up? St. Patrick's soup kitchen."

The bulldog laughed again and turned his gaze back to the ceiling. "Fat Joe don't care 'bout feedin' beggars. 'Sides," he added. "Fat Joe's rich. He could buy food fer the kitchen if he wanted."

"Maybe he's practicing for something big," Lewis said meaningfully.

Scrugg didn't notice. He squished his bulk a little more firmly in the seat. "Nah—them Flash Gang antics were some streeters' doin', I knew. So I was lookin' fer small people." He flicked a glance at Lewis and snorted. "Then I saw you, and it all got real clear. Yer the spittin' image of yer old man—got his hair, his eyeglasses and," Scrugg added with another sneer, "his bleedin' heart."

Scrugg finished, looking quite pleased with himself. Lewis only frowned. He'd taken such pride in not being noticed. So much for that. "So what?" he snapped back. "What did you have to nab me for? You had the notebook—" Then Lewis swallowed, took a risk. "You have my father."

"*Pfft!* The professor refused to do more slag refinin' after he figgered out just what he'd stumbled onto. We had to bring in some'un else. Some'un friendlier."

"The Deutscher," Lewis filled in, remembering. He waited, hoping Scrugg would say something more about his dad. But Scrugg only gazed up at the ceiling, like he was settling in for a long train ride, so Lewis plunged in again. "The Deutscher can refine the slag for you. You don't need me or my dad."

"Ain't so easy, kid. You saw. The Deutscher blew himself up. A bad little accident. An' that was with the original materials. Boss hardly wants some newbie tryin' ta make somethin' from nuthin' with them gobbledygook instructions. But you, kid, you got the original ingredients, all packaged up nice fer us in yer pockets. An' you were making flashes just fine."

"Flashes, not explosions!" Lewis spat. "It wasn't anything like a weapon, like what you're making!"

"Yeah, 'cause ya didn't have the third ingredient. That's all. You understand yer dad's work. I know you got his other pots, all that original stash from his experiment, an' you figgered out them proportions jes' fine." Scrugg gave a self-satisfied sort of nod. "You'll give us the pots, we'll give ya a bit of that third ingredient and let you figure out how to make it all go boom properly."

"Might as well wait for never," Lewis muttered.

Scrugg sighed. "You Carters. All that right versus wrong

stuff gets boring, kid. You'll make us what yer dad refused ta."

"Where is he?" Lewis asked finally, between clenched teeth. "Where's my dad?"

Scrugg didn't pull his smug gaze from the ceiling, and Lewis was about to scream at him to answer when suddenly, without changing his focus, the bulldog offered softly, "Boss liked 'im. I heard him say yer dad had a great mind, say he coulda won a prize for his inventin'." He whistled under his breath, like he was impressed. "Imagine figurin' how to sort a heap of trash inta' somethin' so useful."

Liked. Had. Could've. Past tense. Lewis's throat went dry.

"But no vision, that professor. Too worried 'bout what he'd discovered." Scrugg sighed and cracked his knuckles. "Top-o'-the-line, grade-A ammunition! All free, all from junk that we got a mountain of! Best part is you can fit it to the task! Make a small explosion—" he snickered "—I call thems 'personal.' Or: an explosion so big...*Poof.*" Scrugg spread his fingers to show an imaginary puff of smoke floating away, then shrugged. "Too bad. Yer dad coulda' made a ton of dough. You'd've been rich."

Lewis choked, "So that's what happened? My dad tried to stop your stupid boss from using his experiment as a weapon, so you killed him?" When Scrugg kept chuckling, Lewis threw himself across the aisle at the bulldog, yelling ferociously: "*Tell me!* Is. My. Father. Dead?"

Scrugg's laughter dried up. He lifted Lewis by the elbows and set him back on his seat. Then he made a tiny, awful shrug. "Accidents happen, kid. These are hard times."

All the ferocity left Lewis in one silent exhale. He felt his shoulders sag and then his whole body go limp. And numb. He couldn't feel his eyeglasses slip and his jacket tug as he sank against the unforgiving cushion; he couldn't feel the ropes tightly wound around his hands and feet. He couldn't feel anything, except the razor-sharp scrape of each breath. And he couldn't seem to think of anything, except the window in their second-floor apartment across the river. He'd been waiting for that light to go back on. Now there was nothing to wait for.

"Aw, kid, don't take it hard. Boss says his invention will change the world!"

"Only if I help you. Which I won't," Lewis whispered.

Scrugg stood up and stretched. "Gotta get this engineer to move it." He looked at Lewis. "Don't make your dad's mistakes, kid. It ain't worth it."

Lewis looked up dully, staring straight into Scrugg's beady eyes. A tingle reignited inside, pitting into his stomach and threading through his veins. It was a tingle of unvarnished fury, fury at this bulldog, and the boss, and Nazis, and all of it. He hated them. Every single one. And he wanted nothing more than to make them sorry they'd ever touched his dad, ever tried to make something evil from an innocent experiment. The tingling grew, and expanded, from veins to bones to muscles. And then…

He could yank his wrists free right there, he knew it. He had enough fury to take down the whole train. Lewis gave a smile of pure ice at Scrugg, and Scrugg must have felt it for he blinked, the smugness fading from his ugly face.

Suddenly, there was a lurch and a scream of brakes, and the train dragged to a dead stop. The bulldog went tumbling forward, landing on his belly in the aisle, and Lewis laughed at him.

"What the he—?" Scrugg cursed as he struggled to his feet, shouting toward the front, "What'd ya stop for? Get going!"

The engineer shouted back, "Can't! There's somethin' on the tracks!"

Lewis tore his gaze from the bulldog. He jerked his knees

onto the seat and pushed himself up, leaning over the seat-
back in front of him, trying to see through the engineer's
doorway to the windshield.

"There's something—" the engineer repeated loudly,
sounding very confused. "By golly! Is that a girl?"

"Huh?" Scrugg sounded just as confused.

"That's a girl, all right! She's got on some kind of ballerina
dress! She's just lying on the tracks!"

"Pearl!" Lewis shouted, a surge of pure joy pushing
through all the hate and fury.

"*Shaddap!*" Scrugg barked at Lewis. He marched to the
front and the burlies heaved to their feet, looking murderous-
ly ready to follow orders. "Whaddaya mean, on the tracks?"
he yelled at the engineer.

"See?" the engineer was pointing, astonished. "It's like
that *Lola Lavender* episode, 'Railway Ruckus'! I think she's tied
to the tracks!"

Scrugg grasped the engineer by his uniform and shook
him. "You start that engine, you blockhead. You roll right
over that kid, ya hear?"

"No!" Lewis yelled.

"I can't do that!" protested the engineer.

"Now." Scrugg flashed his jacket open. The thick handle of a pistol stuck out of his belt. He repeated viciously,
"Now."

The engineer backed away and turned to the controls, his
shoulders quivering. Then he stopped dead, peered again
through the windshield. "What the—?"

Scrugg exploded. "Move it!" he ordered, but the engineer
leaned so far forward he nearly pushed through the glass.
"Where'd she go?" he asked. Lewis hung over the seat, trying
desperately to see.

At that moment, a hail of rocks splattered against the carriage windows and then the train car was plunged into chaos.

24

THE BEST RESCUE EVER

The glass smashed. Kids, ten of them at least, came swarming through the windows. Yips and howls exploded in the carriage, and then gravel and pebbles and other debris rained down on everyone.

Lewis couldn't see for all the commotion; neither could anyone else. The burlies spun in circles, the engineer fended off a scrappy five-year-old climbing on his shoulders and Scrugg yelled for the engineer to start the train.

But the kids—they were streeters. Lewis caught glimpses—wasn't that Spike, from Dwight's shoeshine stand? And the one on the engineer, he was Peanut. They charged down the aisle and leaped over the seats, banging sticks as they went and throwing pebbles and shreds of newspaper and any other bits of trash they had stuffed inside their unraveling sweaters and threadbare jackets. They shouted and cheered and jeered, causing such confusion no one could think straight.

Lewis tried to move but fell back on the seat just as a cheerful face loomed into view. "Duck!" he gasped.

"Hey, Brain." Duck grinned. "Mind sitting up a hitch?"

Lewis stared back, astonished. "How did—?"

"Gettin' you outta here. C'mon!" Duck untied both sets of ropes with a couple of flicks of his fingers. Then he grabbed Lewis's elbow and pulled him upright. "Go!" he said, pushing Lewis—not to the aisle, but over the seat. Lewis was hardly able to think. "There!" said Duck. "Clean window!" He meant one with no large shards of glass. "You first!"

Lewis, with a boost from Duck, had got his feet through the empty frame when he heard Scrugg yelling at the burlies. "Idiots! Forget them! Get the *boy*!"

And Lewis gasped, remembering. "The notebook! I need the red notebook!"

"Where?" Duck asked.

"That bulldog's breast pocket!"

"Mac!" Duck shouted. "*Bulldog!* Right flap!"

Duck pushed Lewis through the window. For a moment Lewis hung, propped by his armpits, craning his head to look. Scrugg batted and swatted and raged. And suddenly there was Mac, pinching his dad's notebook from Scrugg's pocket, right under Scrugg's flailing hands. The notebook went sailing across to Duck.

Lewis let go. He landed on the gravelly slope by the tracks and scrambled to his feet. Duck was at the window. "Here!" Duck called and tossed him the notebook.

Lewis, for all his awkwardness, caught it deftly. He hugged it briefly before stuffing it in his jacket. Grateful. And sad.

Duck landed beside Lewis. Mac dove out another window with a whoop and ran to them, socking Lewis in the arm as a greeting. Then Duck gave a sharp whistle and the other streeters vaulted from the carriage, running in every direction.

"Gotta go, Brain! This way!"

Mac led the charge past the rail car and the engine. There, up ahead, was Pearl. Her pink tutu was the color of charcoal, and her bow was no longer bow-shaped, but she still looked like some sort of errant butterfly, flitting with excitement in the middle of the tracks.

"Nigel!" she cried, throwing her arms around Lewis in a bear hug.

"*That*, Pearl Alice Clavell," panted Lewis, squeezing back, "was the *best* rescue *ever*."

"Wasn't it just?" Pearl gloated. "'Railway Ruckus'!" And

Lewis could only smile in return, thinking Lola Lavender had nothing on Pearl.

"Ain't over yet!" cried Duck. "Gotta go, now!"

There was a roar behind them. Scrugg stumbled from the train and pushed the delirious-looking burlies in front of him. "Get 'em! GET 'EM!"

Scrugg neglected to point to which 'em he meant and so two of the burlies went running to the left and right of the tracks, chasing the wrong kids. Mac, Duck, Pearl, and Lewis ran straight ahead on the track.

"Think they'll catch us?" cried Pearl breathlessly.

"Uh…yeah." Mac gulped. "Move it!"

"Here!" called Duck who'd raced ahead. There were stairs, overused, lopsided wooden planks navigating the steep slope from the tracks to Liberty Avenue. Duck pummeled down them, the others right behind. Lewis's lungs were ready to burst.

"Hurry!"

The four charged across the avenue and up barely half a block when Lewis suddenly slowed, then stopped. It wasn't enough, he thought, panting. Even with the notebook he couldn't just run away from this. He couldn't.

The others had come back for him. "C'mon, Brain!"

"Not yet. I have—"

Duck pushed Lewis behind the nearest stoop and they all crowded in.

Lewis looked at his rescuers piled practically on top of his nose. He took a ragged breath. "I'll need your help—"

"Whatever you're plannin', you gotta hurry," burst Mac, glancing anxiously over his shoulder.

"The hoppers—attached to the train—" Words fell out fast. "It's a whole bunch of waste from the steel mills. We need to empty them, right where they're sitting. Right on the tracks." Lewis thought of the engineer's warning about not spilling. If the tracks were buried under the slag, that would get Scrugg and maybe his boss in deep trouble. Lewis's eyes found Pearl's and he gave her a small grin. "Let's mess up these traitors."

"Our very own Nefarious Deed!" breathed Pearl.

Duck stuck his tongue between the gap in his teeth, then grinned. "Sounds fun."

"Guys, the bulldog's coming!" moaned Mac.

Scrugg, along with the third burly, was huffing his way across Liberty Avenue. Lewis said quickly, "I'll slow you down. Go on without me."

"No!" cried Pearl, grabbing Lewis's arms. "Scrugg will find you!"

"Go on, Pearl," Lewis gasped, trying to extricate himself.

"Not without you!" Pearl tugged.

"We gotta move!" Mac insisted.

Duck said, smooth and quick, "St. Patrick's. It's up a block or so. Get there. We'll find you."

"Not the church," Lewis started to say. "It's not open." But Duck and Mac were gone, tearing away down the avenue, making no secret of their escape. The last burly spied them and charged after. However muscled and murderous a burly might be, he'd never catch those two streeters.

"Come on, Nigel," Pearl yanked him out from behind the stoop and pulled him forward.

Lewis wanted to object but he didn't have enough breath. The streets were exposed; streetlights glowed, and a smog-tainted moon was up, revealing more light than shadow. It was eerie how everything seemed to be repeating, Scrugg chasing them all the way to St. Patrick's. It wouldn't be open. They would climb up the grand steps and be stuck, and then Scrugg would be there…

There was a roar from behind. The bulldog thudded up the empty avenue. He was gaining.

Lewis gathered what energy he could muster to match Pearl's pace. Past Sixteenth Street, past the remaining scraps of shantytown debris, and then there was the enormous brick church, looming like a great gray-white shadow. They were at the steps; Pearl dropped his wrist and leaped them two at a time. It was pointless to follow, so Lewis hung back, gasping, trying to think: the steps, the columns—they could maybe run around the church, escape down the alley—

"Come on!" cried Pearl. Lewis looked up.

It was open. St. Patrick's was open. Pearl had pushed wide one of the great doors, revealing a dark rectangle of escape. Lewis burst up the stairs with renewed energy. Together they ran inside and pulled the door shut just as Scrugg started mounting the steps.

"Which way?" said Pearl breathlessly.

Lewis looked around, his chest heaving. "There—go." He prodded Pearl sideways. No use running down the nave or into the back where the rectory and the soup kitchen were. It was too big, too open. Instead, they went up.

To the belfry.

Stairs. Tons more stairs. Lewis clenched his teeth, air hissing through his nose. Pearl followed, half pushing him. The smoggy moonlight that spilled through the windows dissipated, and the stairs and the walls around them narrowed. Far beneath them one of the great doors slammed open and Scrugg roared, "Lewis Carter!" They heard his heavy tread hustling down the aisle, the clunks of something heavy against wood, as if Scrugg was checking the pews.

Lewis immediately regretted not heading for the rectory. Pearl's slippers whispered up the steps, but his boots were another matter. Even his panting was going to give them away. And there was a thick bell rope hanging heavily from above—it released a haunting tone as his shoulder brushed it.

Sure enough, the clunking stopped—Scrugg was listening. And then he roared again and came thudding for the belfry stairs.

"Quick!" Pearl urged.

They'd climbed all the way to the top, crawling through a square opening underneath the great bell and onto a wooden platform. Slatted shutters on all four sides of the tower let in the dimmest of light. Lewis squinted, trying to see where to hide. There were more ropes wound on the floor, a thick layer of soot that settled over everything, and nothing else. Nowhere else.

Lewis swallowed. This was it.

"Get behind me." He went to push Pearl, but she was having none of it.

"You get behind me," she ordered back. "This is my rescue, remember?"

"For Pete's sake! He's going to catch me, Pearl, I'm not fast enough. But you are. So, when he grabs me, just run, will you? Run far away, where your aunt can't find you. And don't come back for me this time. Promise? Blood Oath?"

The tread of Scruggs's boots grew louder. Pearl's chin trembled and her eyes sparkled. "No."

"Come on!" Lewis shook her. "I'm trying to protect you!"

She shook back. "We protect each other, Nigel! We're a team!"

They gripped arms. Soot billowed from beneath their shuffling feet. Lewis could hear Scrugg huffing up the last of the stairs, his breath going *oof, oof, oof.* There was no time left.

"You're right. We're a team, and we will get out of this," he promised fast, and swung around so she was behind him just as Scrugg's flat head appeared in the well beneath the bell.

The beady eyes darted around the gloom. "Well, well… lookee here."

Pearl grabbed Lewis's shoulder, but the bulldog growled, "Don't even think of moving," and aimed something that froze them both in place. It was the pistol.

"Don't shoot!" Pearl gasped.

"Don't make me," Scrugg sneered.

Pearl went silent. Lewis held his breath, all the while

scanning: ropes, slats, soot, and the only escape—the trap door—currently occupied by Scrugg.

Scrugg started to climb the rest of the way into the belfry and promptly knocked his head against the bell. He ducked and swore. Soot swirled up like tiny dust cyclones.

An idea came to Lewis in that moment, an idea spun from the sudden, crazy knowledge that all of Pearl's gobble talk had made terrific sense—because he understood her. He and Pearl shared a code now—not like his father's flowery notes or the streeters' shorthand or even the hobos' scrawls, but something uniquely their own. *We are a team.* Lewis grinned.

"Pearl?" he whispered, under Scrugg's cursing and the hollow, metallic echo of the bell. "Remember 'Tragic Trapeze'?"

Her chin dug in his shoulder as she nodded.

"Good. *Go!*" Lewis flung an arm, pointing to the opposite side of the tower. Pearl leaped from behind Lewis and soared right past Scrugg and the bell, landing more gracefully than she'd ever done before. It was fantastic.

Scrugg whisked his pistol to Pearl. "I said to stay!"

"I'm staying!" Pearl gulped, taking a step back. Lewis kicked a cloud of soot with his foot, then sank to a crouch and reached for his pockets.

Scrugg spluttered and swiped his eyes with his free arm. He swung the pistol toward Lewis, then back at Pearl when she kicked more soot at him. "You made us late," Scrugg growled to both. He struggled onto the platform and stood upright, one hand rubbing the hurt spot on his head. "Makes me look bad in front o' the boss." He squinted back and forth between the two; Lewis's hands kept very still by his knees.

Pearl caught Lewis's eye and gave him the tiniest nod. "The only thing you're late for is jail!" she declared to Scrugg then, gamely.

Lewis eased his father's notebook from his jacket.

"I'll pop you now!" he barked at Pearl. "An' tell yer aunt there was an accident!"

Lewis worked fast, notebook open, fingers slipping out his Recipe pouches. *A smear of sludge, a sprinkle of ash...*

Pearl played her role admirably. "I'll take the third option," she announced with a toss of her head.

Scrugg bellowed, "Shaddap!" The pistol waved and she gulped.

"Hey!" shouted Lewis. He'd shut the red notebook tight and had hidden it behind his back. *Twenty seconds.* He asked, "If you shoot me, who's going to help you with your stupid weapons?"

The bulldog's face contorted in a snarl. He reached for Pearl, but she stepped backward, straight into the wall.

Lewis's heart was in his throat. He clutched the leather binding, the only thing that remained of his dad. Not for much longer. *Fifteen...fourteen...*

Scrugg snarled. "I'm tired o' bein' nice." He pointed the pistol at Pearl but looked at Lewis. "And I'm tired o' you. Period."

There was a silence. Pearl stood bravely straight, though her knees were wobbling. Lewis held where he was, squeezing the notebook hard. *Ten...nine...eight...*

"Say goodbye, girlie," sneered Scrugg, menacingly. He cocked the pistol.

"Wait!" said Lewis loudly. He took a step forward. "I surrender. Take me." *Three...two...*

When Scrugg looked back, Lewis said, "Catch."

He tossed the notebook high, just as there was a small *whoosh* and a soft *pop*. The notebook burst into a dazzling, ballooning, blinding flash of light.

Pearl gasped. Scrugg thundered. The pistol went off.

And suddenly, suddenly, it was no longer a ballooning brilliance, but a spark, a flare, and then the bell tower exploded into flame.

25

THE WORLD ON FIRE

Lewis fell flat on his back. The soot, the ropes, the wooden slats, everything seemed to catch fire at once. Scrugg screamed, and then he was through the trap door and down the steps, faster than any bulldog could ever move. Lewis rolled on the floor smothering the flames that had caught the corduroy of his jacket sleeve. He yelled, terrified, "Pearl!" Had she been hit?

Then, Lewis remembered that Pearl was all in tulle. Shot or not, she would go up like a puff of smoke. "*Pearl!*"

The very air felt scorched. Lewis could barely breathe; his lungs fizzed in panic. Pearl wasn't where she should be, on the opposite side of the platform. He crawled forward. His hands found the edge of the hole of the stairwell. "Pearl!" She had to be somewhere. "Pearl!"

"Lewis!"

Lewis's heart leapt. "Stay down! Crawl toward the bell!"

She was coughing. It was terrible—he was used to so little air, he knew how to salvage every breath, but Pearl was gagging and dragging in huge gulps of hot smoke. "C'mon, Pearl!"

They had only a moment before the tower would be completely consumed. He stretched out his other hand as far as it could go, reaching, desperate, into the red haze. He was surrounded by flames and smoke. The whole world was on fire.

Fingers brushed his. "Here! I'm here!" he shouted. The fingers brushed again; this time Lewis caught her hand and held hard.

"Lewis." Her voice was a thread. There was something awful in the fact that she finally called him by his name.

Lewis said fiercely, "We're getting out of here." He held her fast, and wormed onto his belly, kicking his legs over the side of the stairwell. His feet found the narrow stairs. He tugged on Pearl as he went, and she pretty much fell on top of him. They went tumbling onto the nearest landing, Pearl sprawling like a dead weight on his chest.

"Ow," grunted Lewis. He felt Pearl move a little, start to sit up. He squirmed out from under and got to his hands and knees, gasping, "Are you hurt? Are you shot?" He could barely see, his eyeglasses were coated with ash. But Pearl squeezed his hand, coughed up a bunch of soot, and spit it out. Just like him, he thought crazily.

"That," she rasped, wiping her mouth, "was better than *any* Lola Lavender episode."

Lewis, despite everything, started laughing.

Pearl smiled her brilliant smile, white teeth in a smoke-smeared face. Then her eyes widened. She looked like she was going to announce the most amazing thing. "And *you!* When were—?"

The moment was interrupted. A shower of sparks rained down from the belfry. The soot on the landing immediately leaped into flame, catching the wooden stair.

"The whole tower is going up!" Lewis shouted. "We gotta go!"

They scrambled down the next set of stairs and the next. And when the stairwell got wider, they clasped hands and went side by side, fast as they could. The smoke funneled down from the steeple, pouring into the church. Sparks whizzed past like fireflies, catching fire where they landed. Flames rippled across the ceiling, outlining windowpanes.

There was an exit to the side, past the chancel. They wrapped their sleeves around their noses and ran toward it.

The door popped open and a blast of heat and smoke

pushed them outward. Lewis and Pearl stumbled down steps into the alley and staggered toward the entrance to the street. Then they simply sank to their knees, stunned by what they saw.

A crowd was gathering on the sidewalks of Liberty Avenue and Seventeenth Street. Faces glowed in the flickering light, eyes turned upward. The steeple of St. Patrick's was crumbling to ash above them, flames eating the roof. Fire trucks had lined up around the church. Arcs of water shot into the sky, evaporating on contact. Firemen scurried up ladders and down ladders, pulled hoses, and shouted over the thunderous blaze. The crowd groaned as each burning timber plummeted into the building.

Lewis nudged Pearl. "Look," he whispered.

A group of coppers was restraining a wild Scrugg. One of the coppers had Scrugg's pistol, three held his arms, while a fourth wrangled a pair of handcuffs around his wrists. Scrugg was shouting all the while—Lewis caught, "Kids!" "Made me!" and "Flash Gang!" and lots of other things that sounded like desperate excuses. Lewis smiled, if briefly. It didn't look good for Scrugg, but it was very good for them.

"Any kids in that fire?" one of the coppers yelled to another.

"Three adults safe. That's it. No kids."

The first copper said to Scrugg, "You better hope we don't find no dead kids, or you'll be up for arson *and* murder."

Pearl whispered, "Look, there's Mac. And Duck."

Sure enough, the two streeters, both smeared with what looked like a good bit of slag, were visible in the crowd. They were close enough to have heard the police say, "No kids…Murder," for they stood gaping in shock. For once, they weren't even pinching.

Pearl whispered anxiously, "We've got to get to them!"

She started to move, but Lewis touched her sleeve, shook his head. Scrugg could *not* see him and Pearl. And anyway,

Mac and Duck were already slipping through the crowd like shadows. A moment later they'd completely vanished.

"What do we do?" asked Pearl.

"I guess we'll play dead for a night or two," Lewis replied. "Come on."

Together they slipped back into the alley, found a loose board in a fence, and crawled through. A block farther and they, too, were just another set of shadows in the smoggy, smoky Pittsburgh night. In silence they walked past sagging houses with neatly swept front steps, sleeping men clustered in corners, trolley lines that carried folks to jobs they were desperate to keep, and the few sleek automobiles that whisked crusts through their fancy world.

"Lewis. *Lewis.*"

It was the second time that evening she had called him by his name. Lewis looked over his shoulder.

Pearl had stopped. Her arms were crossed. "When?"

Lewis stopped.

"*When* were you planning on telling me about being a member—" Pearl lowered to a whisper "—of the Flash Gang?"

Lewis stood very still. There was so much to say, but how could he tell Pearl all he needed to right there—not just about the Flash Gang, and the Recipe, and how it all happened, but about his father too? How could he, with a raw throat and adrenaline dissipating, leaving him shaky and cold and bone tired?

Pearl didn't seem to feel any of his exhaustion. She stalked around him in a circle. "You realize, of course, that I knew. Right from the start, by the way. I am an *expert* detective. I was merely allowing you to choose the perfect moment. But despite our Blood Oath and our near-death experiences, you didn't say anything! So." Pearl looked around. "Where's the rest of the gang? Where does everyone hide?"

"I'm it," said Lewis simply. "There isn't anyone else."

Pearl went very still. "Huh?"

"*I* am the Flash Gang," he said. Then he gave her a lop-sided grin that was maybe…maybe just the tiniest bit smug. After all, her detective expertise—for all its worth—had not detected that.

Pearl stood for a long moment, her breath sighing out in an "*Ohhhhhh…*"

Maybe that said it all. Lewis turned with his own sigh. "C'mon, Pearl. Let's go home."

26

A Gang, at Last

The walk downtown was different than it had been yesterday. For one thing, there were no stringy bits clogging Lewis's lungs, and no worry that a bulldog in a green suit might suddenly appear to kidnap him. True, his belly was empty, and his heart was broken in a way that would never heal, but the sun was very bright that morning, piercing through the usual gloom as if it refused to completely surrender. And that seemed a hopeful sign.

Besides, he wasn't alone.

"How I wish we could spy on Aunt Gimlick," Pearl said between hops over the sidewalk cracks. "She'll be in the most *ferocious* mood because we've outwitted her! Her face turns the color of her skirts when she's angry."

"You know we can't go back to your aunt's house. It's not safe."

Pearl hopped. "Well, yes. Although we—ow!"

A crust with fashionable hair and a mink stole pushed between Pearl and Lewis, her heavy purse knocking Pearl in the elbow as she passed.

"Excuse yourself!" Pearl shouted. She started to charge after the woman, but Lewis grabbed her.

"Hey!" he said under his breath. "She didn't notice you! It worked!"

Pearl beamed at that, and then looked down to admire her getup. They'd exchanged all the pink things for Lewis's spare britches and knee socks. Lewis had torn her ribbon so it was no longer a bow, but a strip to tie up her hair under an old knit cap. Last night's soot still smudged her cheeks and nose.

In fact, the only hint of the perfect Pearl from two days back was the ballet slippers.

"These won't do," Pearl said, frowning at her toes while Lewis continued ahead. "I beg you to reconsider, Nigel. All it would take is one little—"

"Nope," called Lewis.

Pearl ran to catch up. "Please? I am absolutely desperate to watch you make the…" She made some fluffy gestures with her hands.

"No."

"I could pinch real boots, then. I'd be completely disguised."

"You were just ignored with slippers!" Lewis reminded her. "And I don't have any with me, *and* we already agreed: no"—he hissed it very low—"Flash."

"I know, but—"

And then they turned the corner and were on the block of the shoeshine stand, and all that Pearl had been about to say was lost at the sight of Fat Joe and Dwight in the midst of their eleven o'clock routine. Lewis and Pearl ducked under the shadow of a broad awning just as Dwight whistled, and then they watched the arrival of the sleek Ford and subsequent departure of the mobster. It was as impressive as it had been yesterday. Dwight even caught the mobster's coin in his cap.

As the henchboss settled against his postbox, Pearl said under her breath, "You know, we could search Fat Joe's den, just like we did Mr. Scrugg's office. I'll bet there will be proof connecting him to Aunt Gimlick and the evil boss in there."

"We'll do it just like we discussed," Lewis answered firmly, then grinned. "For today, at least." And then Lewis, with Pearl close behind, left the shadow of the awning and walked casually down the street toward the shoeshine stand.

"Look," said Pearl.

Two streeters, one tall and one jittery, had just arrived

at the stand. They were waving the morning *Post-Gazette* at Dwight and pelting him with questions.

"Have you heard anything from Brain?"

"What about the wise guy—Scrugg—how long's he in jail for?"

Mac and Duck couldn't read; they wanted Dwight to tell them what the paper said.

"What about how the train stopped?"

"What about Pearl? They find bodies?"

Dwight chewed his toothpick.

"'Course they didn't find bodies, Mac!" Duck snorted. "I'm tellin' ya, they nicked out of the church in time."

"Are you nuts? Look at this picture!" Mac said, ruffling the newspaper to show a dark photo and what was clearly a big headline. "We're talkin' 'bout Lewis. Slower than cold molasses!"

"I am not!" replied Lewis stoutly, stopping a few yards from them.

Everyone except Dwight whipped around in surprise. "Holy cow!" "Brain!" "You're alive!" Mac and Duck—even Peanut and Spike, who'd been lounging in the shoeshine seats—flew to greet him.

"Careful!" laughed Lewis, collapsing as Duck hung on his shoulders. "I just survived a fire, don't squish me to death!" Duck let go and Mac immediately socked him.

"How'd you beat—Whoa!" Mac turned crimson as he recognized Pearl. "You...you're...different!"

"Yes," said Pearl very seriously. "I am incognito."

"In...where?"

"Hiding, Sir Mac," said Pearl. "We are but two steps from the clutches of evil."

"Uh...what?" asked Mac, redder than ever.

Just then, Dwight whistled and everyone stopped. A crust had plopped into one of the vacated shoeshine seats. Spike rushed to attend him.

"You two need work today?" the henchboss called out to Mac and Duck. "Shoot or get lost. You're makin' a scene."

Duck replied cheerfully enough, "Can't do nothin' but listen to their story! Come on, Dwight, don't you wanna hear it?"

"Can't say as I do."

"Oh, honestly." Sounding miffed that the henchboss was not glued to what would obviously be a death-defying tale, Pearl snatched the newspaper from Mac and cried, "Follow me, gentlemen. I shall reveal all of our very own, infamous—" she paused, then named it like a Lola Lavender episode: "—'Fiery Flight'!" Pearl strode partway down the block, the streeters in tow, and began to re-enact their story of escape, playing all parts, including the church, with great theatrical detail. Peanut, looking crestfallen, loyally remained behind with Dwight.

This was as good an opportunity as any, Lewis figured. He cleared his throat. "Say, Dwight, do you think Peanut could, um, get the news for me?" As payment for the favor, Lewis pulled his last tin of ham out of his jacket pocket and handed it over.

Dwight considered the ham, then tossed it to Peanut with an offhand nod. Peanut scurried off like a mouse. Dwight turned back to Lewis and gave him that appraising look that made it seem the henchboss knew everything about him. He said offhandedly, "Fetched a Buick this mornin', over by the Pickering factory. Changed a tire, but it drives fine."

Lewis flushed. "Yeah, I'm going to apologize for that."

Dwight squinted up, studied the sunshine. "I ain't in the habit of giving out tips," he said after a moment. "But save your sorrys till you really owe 'em. A stolen car ain't nearly enough to trouble Osgood Boone, and me and my boys can handle trickier jobs than that."

Lewis nodded, then said carefully, "Pearl says you had a lot to do with getting all the streeters to help stop the train.

Thanks. Really. I sure didn't know what I was going to do."

"You'da come up with somethin'. You're a bold kid."

It was a compliment, a huge one, coming from the likes of Dwight. Lewis felt his chest swell ever so slightly.

Dwight stretched, scratched a spot beneath his cap. "Here." He slid his hand into his leather jacket and pulled out the green and gold brooch. "Give this back to your friend," he said, dropping it into Lewis's upturned palm. "Emeralds are too valuable to fence, and I don't take family heirlooms unless I gotta. But," he said, straightening, "so we're clear, I'm runnin' a tab for you two and your 'favors.' It'll take a lot more than ham."

Lewis looked up from the brooch, stunned. "Wha—?"

But Dwight was already walking toward the entrance to Fat Joe's lair. "Can't hang here, Lewis Carter," he called over his shoulder. "They'll be lookin'. Wait outside the Brass Rail."

And then the henchboss disappeared into Fat Joe's den, leaving Spike furiously polishing a crust's shoes, and Lewis holding a brooch and several questions.

Lewis studied the brooch, then rubbed it on his corduroy jacket. Family heirloom?

He looked down the block at Pearl, who was staggering back and forth, her hands clutched at her throat, while Mac and Duck gaped, transfixed. It occurred to Lewis as he watched that Pearl, for all her exaggerations, never lied. Not really. She stretched the truth a bit—okay, a lot—to make things more entertaining, but she never outright made things up.

Lewis watched, thinking about what Pearl had said about her papa, and his background, and his supposed resources and exotic trips—

A memory struck him then, like a bolt of lightning, and Lewis gasped. It was of his dad reading aloud from the newspaper about an eccentric millionaire, a distant cousin of somebody related to the king of England, a member of some super crusty, hoity-toity Explorers Club. A Sir Thaddeus Clavell. The name and title had not impressed Lewis or his dad, but the recount of crystal caves and ancient tombs and Amazon adventures had sounded just like the *Tarzan* movie. "I'd sure like to speak with this gentleman!" his dad had mused, fascinated. "Do you know that there are creatures living in those jungles that the world has never seen? Imagine the science!"

An automobile zoomed past, startling Lewis back into the present. He swallowed and carefully stowed the memory away, then looked down again and traced the gem with his finger. It glinted. Like a wink. "Unbelievable," Lewis sighed, shaking his head. A moment later he slipped the jewel into the front right pocket of his corduroy jacket, where there was normally a little sack of ash. Then he headed down the block and told Pearl, Mac, and Duck to follow him.

They walked to the Brass Rail restaurant, with its shiny brass door handles and enticing smell. The four planted themselves outside and Pearl waved Mac's newspaper at Lewis. "Here. It's on the front page!"

Lewis adjusted his glasses. He could see the sad photo of a burned and half-crumbled structure with the headline: "Flames Destroy Popular Pittsburgh Church." "Poor St. Patrick's," he said.

"Not that—look!"

She unfolded the paper, revealing another, smaller headline: "Pickering & Lowe Faulted for Morning Train Delays."

"That's us!" Duck boasted, tucking his hands into the front of his overalls. "We left a whole lotta slag to scoop off the track!"

"Nearly got caught by some burlies," Mac added pompously. "Pearl says the paper reports those crusty factory owners are gonna get slapped with a big fine!"

"Serves 'em right," agreed Duck.

Pearl shook her head, impatiently. "No, no, not that! This!"

She stabbed the very bottom of the page, where a much, much smaller headline and photograph announced, "Benefactor Contributes to City Improvements." "It's the evil boss," she crowed.

Yesterday Lewis would have dismissed Pearl's enthusiasm. Today he pulled the paper close. At first glance, the article was just a boring list of a rich businessman's philanthropy. The photo was of two crusts, one tall, one stout, stiffly shaking hands. Below, a tiny headline announced the creation of a Fund for Pittsburgh, by the richest man in Pittsburgh, Mr. John J. Pickering, owner of Pickering & Lowe Steel.

Lewis considered the photo again. The taller man had to be Mr. Pickering, since he looked the richest. He had on a dark overcoat; there was silvery-gray hair under his fedora. Lewis focused on the clasped hands.

Pickering wore a gold signet pinkie ring.

"See it?" Pearl murmured.

"I see it," he murmured back.

"We have a name now, an entire consortium of Nefarious Deed plotters!" Pearl's whispering grew more excited. "Of course, we have to track down more clues, but we shall persevere to bring these menacing, murdering traitors to justice!"

"Eh, what's she on about, Brain?" Mac's face was full of earnestness trying to understand Pearl.

Pearl looked over at Mac and smiled so widely that Mac looked like he might burst apart from blushing. "Now, Nigel," she announced cryptically. "It's time."

Lewis folded the paper. "Sure, Pearl. Have at it."

Pearl reached out a hand each to Mac and Duck, and in her best conspirator voice announced, "Gentlemen, Sir Nigel and I have a proposition, a once-in-a-lifetime opportunity. It will require tremendous valor, utmost secrecy, daring deeds. Oh, and a Blood Oath."

That was met with a pair of baffled expressions.

"We," Pearl continued grandly, gesturing at herself and Lewis, "are going undercover."

Duck started laughing. "What for?" He jerked a thumb at some passersby. "No one sees us."

"Not like streeters," Lewis explained. "More invisible. Like…dead. Like what you thought happened to us in the fire. And we'll need to keep it that way—for a while at least—because, well, we destroyed something of great value to some people who want to—"

Pearl interrupted him, breathless. "The kidnappers of Sir Nigel are involved in evil endeavors."

Mac and Duck looked blank again, and Lewis said, "She means they're up to no good."

"They *must* be stopped," Pearl added nobly. "We are going to stop them."

"Yeah?" Duck looked interested. "How?"

"Er, we don't have an exact plan. Yet," said Lewis, to which Pearl looked offended.

"I have a plan," she insisted. "I have many plans. First—"

Lewis jumped in. "Yes, well, in the meantime we need help." He suddenly felt a little embarrassed. "You know, pinching and such."

Mac narrowed his eyes. "So, what's in it for us?"

Lewis glanced at Pearl. Pearl said blithely, "Nigel and I make the very best lookouts."

"You gonna do the whistlin'?" Duck looked amused.

"I don't whistle very well," Lewis agreed. "But my coughs are pretty recognizable." Pearl then pursed her lips together and whistled so shrilly, everyone cringed. "Or…" Lewis added hastily. "She can."

Mac looked suspicious. "So you want us to pinch food for ya, and you give us, what, exactly?"

"Adventures, Mac! Fun." Duck shrugged. "Wasn't stopping that train the best thing to happen all week?"

Lewis added, "There's also a warm—well, sort of warm—place to stay."

"A secret hideout!" Pearl clarified.

This seemed to interest Mac considerably, so Lewis embellished. "Lots of room. No crusts or coppers or any grown-ups around."

"Absolutely not," Pearl confirmed. "Except for Nazis. There will be plenty of those. Nigel and I shall tell you more, but first comes the Blood Oath, in which you have to swear fealty to our team"—Pearl shot out a hand to stop Lewis from interrupting—"because this is terribly dangerous. You might be tortured."

Everyone stood looking at each other. "Neat," pronounced Duck after a moment.

"How bloody is that oath?" Mac asked a little hesitantly.

"It isn't," said Lewis. "Pinkie shake."

He lifted his finger and offered it. Pearl immediately held hers out. Mac and Duck followed. And then it was a little awkward, four people trying to clasp pinkies at once, but they figured it out. Lewis was the last to let go. There was something special about this moment. He'd lost his dad, but he'd gained friends. And while it didn't take all the hurt away, it took a lot of it away. And he felt pretty special.

Farther down the block he could see Peanut skipping toward them with the reporter, Osgood Boone, hustling behind.

"So, if we're a gang," Duck was saying, "we'll have to have a name."

"A name." Lewis looked at Pearl. She beamed so widely and made such twitches with her nose it looked like it might fall right off. A name for a gang.

"Well, it just so happens…" Lewis took what felt like a very full breath and grinned back at Pearl. "We have got the perfect name for a gang."

Don't miss

The Adventures of the Flash Gang

Episode Two: Treasonous Tycoon

It's been a year since Lewis and Pearl survived a near fatal fire and the evil clutches of Floyd Scrugg, henchman of Pittsburgh's wealthiest steel baron. Together with friends Mac and Duck, they are the new, expanded Flash Gang, complete with a secret hideout and a radio to hear the latest adventures of Lola Lavender. Only problem is, there isn't a flash in sight. Lewis refuses to use his Recipe for any pinching, at least not until he and his friends put the formidable steel baron in jail both for his part in the death of Lewis's father and his efforts to arm the nation's Nazi sympathizers. Besides, he and Pearl are supposed to be dead!

But bigger problems loom: Streeters are vanishing in alarming numbers. It's not just due to the police, who have cracked down on homeless orphans of late. Something far more menacing is afoot, something that threatens to break the bond between the members of Flash Gang. And when Pearl's flashy father shows up, the gang faces their biggest challenge yet: will their friendship survive?

Can't wait? Turn the page for a sneak peek of the first part of *The Adventures of the Flash Gang, Episode Two: Treasonous Tycoon...*

1

Lewis Carter was about to steal something.

Of course, to a streeter, it was considered pinching, not stealing. And for any twelve-year-old who lived on the street during this terrible Depression, pinching was necessary. After all, a meal couldn't be conjured from thin air and it wasn't as if Lewis could saunter into a shop, pick up a tin of sardines and a loaf of bread, then count out the fifteen cents to give the grocer. He had no change; for Pete's sake, he certainly did not have fifteen cents. Very few people had fifteen cents these days.

Still, for Lewis, pinching or stealing or whatever anyone else wanted to call it was a pretty big deal.

"You got this, Brain. Like we talked about," encouraged his friend Duck. He stood behind Lewis, hands on shoulders, aiming him at the target: the kitchen door of a restaurant across the street.

"They're on the counter?" Lewis asked for the third time.

"On a tray," repeated Duck. "I saw 'em. Twenty-four baked potatoes, all salted 'n buttered. Lots 'n lots of butter." He squeezed Lewis's shoulder, trying to coax some courage out of him. "Ya scurry in, pinch two, ya leave!"

Lewis swallowed. "And if they're not there—"

"Then grab what is there. Easy as pie. Like we been practicin'."

Just staring at the restaurant's back door made Lewis's stomach growl. Unfortunately, it also made his lungs start to fizz, which happened whenever Lewis grew anxious.

Truth be told, he was not a good thief.

Even before the city of Pittsburgh began cracking down on homeless kids, even before the coppers stood lookout with their determined and now almost supernatural ability to catch streeters in mid-pinch, Lewis had been anxious about pinching—at least pinching the normal way, with quick hands and speedy feet. Despite Duck's helpful pointers ("Maybe don't look so guilty,") his cohort Mac's less than helpful pointers ("Just go faster!") and his best friend Pearl's very unhelpful pointers ("You must slide along the aisle on your belly like Lola Lavender in 'Surreptitious Secret,'") Lewis was pretty much the worst at it. He was too slow and too easy to identify, thanks to his eyeglasses. Mac and Duck were excellent pinchers, nearly invisible to the vigilant coppers. And Pearl was, well, Pearl.

"Yer the one says ya gotta do this, Brain," Duck was saying. "None of us care!"

"I care," Lewis replied. He did care, too much. When he'd invited Duck and Mac to share his secret hideout, he'd expected to pick up their tricks. One whole year after they'd come together, and Lewis hadn't so much as pinched a gunny sack for their supply closet. This had to change.

"Okay," he said, firmly. "I'm going. Is the coast clear?"

Duck looked left, then right. "Yep." He snickered. "Only coppers 'round here are on Fat Joe's payroll anyway." He nudged Lewis toward the curb.

Lewis took a fizzy breath, stepped into the street, and nearly collided with a lady riding a bicycle who'd just turned the corner.

"Eeek!" she screamed.

"Sorry!" Lewis shouted. The bicycle brakes screeched, Lewis tipped sideways, and a tomato went flying from the sack of groceries in the handlebar basket and splatted hard on the pavement.

Duck grabbed Lewis by the sleeve and yanked him onto the sidewalk as the lady honked her bike horn. "You reckless hooligans!" she huffed. "Running about the streets wasting my hard-earned money!"

"He said he was sorry!" Duck said gamely.

More honking. "A good swat across your backside is what you deserve! I'm calling Child Services!" The lady pedaled away, flattening the tomato, and sent a last glare over her shoulder.

"Don't mind her," said Duck when she was far enough away, but it was too late.

"Let's get out of here," Lewis muttered.

"Aw. Ya sure ya wanna walk away from this one? You're so close!"

Lewis shook his head. "You go on. Today isn't my day."

Duck scratched the side of his face, looking faintly disappointed—not in Lewis, but for Lewis, and Lewis nearly blushed. A whole year! Duck knew this restaurant, how easy it was to snag a potato, and that the coppers here worked for Fat Joe, the biggest mobster in Pittsburgh who had a soft spot for streeters anyway. Duck had picked it especially for Lewis because Lewis kept insisting that he could do this.

Thankfully Duck didn't give him a chance to make more excuses. "See ya at home then," he said cheerfully. "Don't get nabbed!" Then Duck zipped across the street fast as a breeze, and before Lewis blinked, he disappeared into the kitchen door of the restaurant.

Don't get nabbed? Lewis stood watching the store for a moment, feeling useless, his hands jammed in the empty pockets of his corduroy jacket.

His pockets hadn't always been empty. And he hadn't always felt so useless.

Only a year before, he, Lewis Carter, had been the most notorious and mysterious food-thief in all of Pittsburgh.

Things were a lot different now. For everybody.

He turned and started walking, heading up Smallman Street along the Allegheny River, listening for sirens and sticking to the shadows of the buildings—not that there were many shadows on this smoggy gray afternoon. At Twenty-Seventh, he crossed the street to where a makeshift newsstand leaned against a rickety fence. The fence was plastered with ads, wanted posters, the day's news, and scrawls of chalk marks. Lewis gave the fence a cursory glance and continued, only to freeze a moment later as a chill ran down his spine.

The news. That photo. It wasn't possible. It couldn't be…

He approached the fence to get a closer look, dread building with each step. "Church Arsonist Given Early Release," the headline read.

Lewis gasped.

And then, as if the very news had conjured him, a heavy hand slammed down on his shoulder, fat fingers gripping, tugging him around. And suddenly, Lewis was staring in horror at the real-life bulldog, at those squinty eyes, and that nasty leer that still gave him nightmares. His lungs fizzed like firecrackers; he scrabbled at his pockets, frantically trying to reach his pouches, his Recipe, then kicking himself as he remembered there was nothing there. He had no escape.

The squat face loomed closer, the leer widened.

"Miss me?" grinned Scrugg.

The Adventures of the Flash Gang
Episode Two: Treasonous Tycoon
in stores January 2024

ACKNOWLEDGMENTS

We have loved setting our tale against a historical backdrop and have included many real-life settings and events, but this is after all a story, and we could not help but embellish some details, collapse some distances and timelines, and, in general, fudge a bit to tell a good one. We ourselves are not in possession of Lewis's secret Flash Recipe.

We are beyond grateful to those who have supported and cheered and believed in us along the way: our husbands, Jonathan and Chris, writers' groups cohorts, authors Lauren Lipton and Tatiana Boncompagni, Rebecca Caprara and Erin Cashman. Jenny Bent of The Bent Agency and Susan Hawk of Upstart Crow Literary set us on our path, while author and friend Diana Renn was beyond generous with her guidance. Most especially we wish to thank Jaynie Royal, editor-in-chief, publisher, and founder at Regal House, managing editor Pam Van Dyk, and the entire Regal House/ Fitzroy Books team. We feel profoundly privileged to be working with such a wonderful group of women.